D0613844

HIRED BY THE UNEXPECTED BILLIONAIRE

HIRED BY THE UNEXPECTED BILLIONAIRE

SUSAN MEIER

MILLS & BOON

First published in Great Britain 2020
by Mills & Boon, an imprint of HarperCollins*Publishers*
1 London Bridge Street, London, SE1 9GF

Large Print edition 2020

© 2020 Linda Susan Meier

ISBN: 978-0-263-08531-0

MIX
Paper from
responsible sources
FSC™ C007454

This book is produced from independently certified FSC™ paper to ensure responsible forest management. For more information visit www.harpercollins.co.uk/green.

Printed and bound in Great Britain
by CPI Group (UK) Ltd, Croydon, CR0 4YY

The most fitting end to a series
about family is to
dedicate the final book to mine.
Ten siblings, hundreds (only a slight
exaggeration) of nieces and nephews
and great-nieces and great-nephews.
I love you all.

CHAPTER ONE

A SECRET WAS a funny thing. A person could totally forget the worst part of her past, build a new life and be perfectly content, only to have fear turn her blood to ice water when a memory burst in her brain.

She'd been here before.

Marnie Olsen cautiously stepped into Manhattan's Shutto Building, her heart pounding. Brushed metal handrails enhanced the open stairway on the right. Sleek, sophisticated silver cylinders hung from the high ceiling, lighting the lobby. The dark, delicious scent of coffee floated out from Caffeine Burst, a coffee shop on the left. A doorman in a black sweater over a white shirt and red tie stood by a shiny desk. It was early July, but the air-conditioning was cranked up to high. Probably so he could wear the fancy sweater.

She took a breath, forcing away her fear. It had been ten years. Roger Martin wouldn't be here. Even if his father still worked on the nineteenth floor, Roger should have his own job by now. Hopefully in a building far, far away. Plus, the odds of her seeing him were slim. She'd be in and out of her interview in less than an hour.

Shaky but determined, she strode to the desk and the doorman. "I'm Marnie Olsen. I have an interview with Attorney Manelli at Waters, Waters and Montgomery. He said you'd point me to the private elevator and give me the code."

The older man frowned and walked from behind the desk. "*I'll* punch in the code."

She smiled. "Great."

But her confidence took a direct hit. Danny Manelli had told her the elevator code changed hourly. The doorman could have given it to her and by the time her interview was over, it would be different. But no. He saw her simple summer blazer and scuffed shoes and didn't assume she'd just worked her way through university. He saw trash. A low-class woman trying for a high-class job.

Embarrassment heated her face. She hadn't always been poor. She was the daughter of Eddie Gouse, Manhattan real estate mogul. But he'd packed his things and taken her brother, leaving her mom desperately broke with a twelve-year-old daughter to raise. That, in Marnie's mind, was the real beginning of her secret.

The doorman punched in the code and took another look at her before he sniffed in derision and walked away.

As the elevator door closed, she pulled in a shivery breath. She'd literally thought her life was over, thought there was no way she'd ever pass a company's investigatory process to get a job. Then she'd found nannying. The *service* investigated all their applicants. She'd spilled the details of her life once. They vetted her, discovered her secret and cleared her. As long as she worked for them, no one else had to look into her past. Her secret stayed locked away. And she had a nice, secure job from which she could eventually make a nice, secure life.

There was nothing to worry about.

In seconds, Danny Manelli's private elevator arrived at his office. Before the door opened, Marnie composed herself, prayed to relax and pasted a smile on her face.

The panels slowly slid apart and the office beyond, though decorated with shiny oak furniture, was empty, except for a puppy standing on the chair, his front paws on the desk, his head down as if he were reading the document in front of him.

"Well, Mr. Manelli. You're certainly not what I expected."

"What were you expecting?"

The masculine voice from the left made her jump. She pressed her hand to her chest, not knowing whether to die of embarrassment or laugh because she'd been caught talking to a dog.

She chose dignity and turned, offering her hand. "Mr. Manelli?"

But when she raised her gaze to meet his, her heart stuttered. Tall and slim, with perfectly cut short black hair and piercing dark eyes, he was polished but also sexy and male. She could picture him in a bedroom lit only by a few white candles, pouring wine into expensive flutes, turning lovemaking into an art.

She blinked. *Where the heck had that come from?*

"Yes. I'm Danny Manelli. And you must be Marnie Olsen, my two o'clock nanny interview."

"Yes."

He shook her hand once, a crisp movement, before he released her and walked to his desk. He picked up the puppy. "Oswald, we've talked about this. Your bachelor's degree isn't enough.

You have to go to law school and pass the bar before you can edit documents."

His sense of humor surprised her. The puppy wiggled around in his arms until his pink tongue could reach Danny Manelli's face. Then he licked his clean-shaven chin. His tail wagged. His fat tummy jiggled with the frenetic movement. He didn't seem to know what to do with his big paws.

Marnie put her fingers to her lips to hold back a laugh. They were quite a pair. The gorgeous executive and the wiggly puppy. Except—

Oswald? She frowned. He definitely had the dog's name wrong.

"That dog's not an Oswald."

Danny Manelli looked at her as if she'd stolen his last cookie. "Excuse me?"

"He's a Wiggles," she said, walking over to pet the puppy. His ears perked up. His tail wagged wildly. His oversize paws hung over Danny's forearms. Considering their size, Oswald/Wiggles had to be a yellow Lab.

"You're a Wiggles, aren't you, sweetie?" She took the furry ball of energy from his owner, and the dog rewarded her with what felt like eighty rapid-fire chin licks. "Oh, and I see someone hasn't gone to obedience school."

"I had a dog as a child. He never went to obedience school."

"Where'd you live?"

"Upstate."

She winced. "Small-town living is very different than Park Avenue. You'll be taking Wiggles for walks with your little boy. He's going to see other dogs. Run into people he doesn't know. As playful as he is," she said, as the dog enthusiastically squirmed in her arms, "he's going to make contact, and when he does, it might not always end well."

"I thought you were a nanny."

"I am."

"Not a dog expert."

His cool voice sent fear shivering through her again. Danny Manelli was offering three times her usual fee for this job and she needed the money. She also liked the idea that this assignment could turn permanent. She didn't want to lose it over a throwaway comment.

"Lots of the people I worked for were dog owners. That's why I'm familiar with the system."

"Then maybe you should train him?"

The fear rose again. She hated that she was so uncomfortable around new people. She could blame Roger Martin. Let her dread take over and apologetically stumble her way through the interview—

Instead, she forgot all that, raised her chin and looked Danny Manelli in the eye. This was her dream assignment. After a few months of probation, she could have full-time employment. It could mean working with the same child the whole way through his teen years, getting to know him and his family, while making enough money to set some aside. She refused to let it slip through her fingers.

"That's a job for a pro."

"You're telling me I need to hire someone?"

"Or enroll him in a school. There are some excellent choices. I can get you a list."

"I guess I'll have to take you up on that."

Her muscles relaxed. Her breathing returned to normal. For a few seconds, neither spoke. Danny Manelli studied her face as if trying to determine her honesty. Or maybe because nobody had ever told him what to do. Whatever his reason, she stood still under his scrutiny. If he assessed character from a person's face, she would give him time to realize she might be nervous, but she was honest.

Danny reached for the puppy and she handed him over. "Please sit." He pointed to the seat across from his desk. "Excuse my lack of focus. The past few months my life sort of imploded."

"Discovering you're the parent of a two-year-old would be difficult."

"It's more than that." He put the pup on a small dog bed at his feet and gave him a chew toy. "And if you're going to work for me you need to know."

"Okay."

"I was recently told I was adopted."

"Oh."

"I now have a biological father who wants to be in my life, as well as adoptive parents who raised me, who deserve the place my biological father is usurping."

"That's awkward."

"You don't know the half of it." He shook his head. "My biological father is Mark Hinton."

Her mouth fell open. "Mark Hinton? The guy who faked his death?"

"He claims he didn't. That his boat had stalled, and he got himself to safety and never saw the news or went on the internet for the months he was gone."

"Wow."

"Oh, that's just the tip of the iceberg. He's a lot like a tornado. When he comes in, he crashes into everything. And he brings an entourage of bodyguards. Everyone in the family has them now. Nosy and ridiculous as he is, he dug into my personal life, found my son and decided that was reason enough to upend the lives of at least eight people."

Marnie sat back, not knowing what to say. As someone who had worked in other people's homes, seen other people's problems up close and personal without ever getting involved, she would normally answer with something neutral and benign. But this was an interview and, undoubtedly, he wanted her reaction to what he'd said about his father, the *infamous* Mark Hinton.

But for the life of her, she couldn't think of an appropriate response. Her mom was an alcoholic, her dad a real estate mogul accustomed to everyone doing his bidding. When living with her mom had become embarrassing, he'd packed up himself and her brother and gone. He'd wanted Marnie to come with them, but she'd stayed, one more day, unable to leave her unconscious mom for fear she'd die. The next morning when her mom had awakened, still not quite sober, she couldn't reach her husband—who wasn't answering her calls—and she'd shattered into a million tiny pieces. She'd found an A.A. meeting and she'd been sober since.

Yet her dad hadn't come home. He'd also refused to see Marnie or let Marnie see her little brother. He'd called her a defector.

She cleared her throat. "I know a bit about parental drama."

"This isn't drama. This is a man who comes in and takes over people's lives. You'll be dealing with him."

She chuckled. "I'll be fine. Without breaking confidences, I can tell you I've handled a few difficult grandparents. Plus, one of the big perks of being a nanny is that I can always take the child and retreat to the nursery. It's a subtle but effective way of showing an adult like a grandparent that if he missteps, he loses time with the child he came to see."

Danny smiled—his first real smile since she'd entered the room—and it transformed his face, melting the severe lines in his forehead and around his mouth. "That's perfect."

Her heart flipped over in her chest. Attraction rippled through her, surprising her. Though she'd dated on and off in the six years she'd been at university, it had been a long, long time since she'd had an instinctive reaction like this. Part lust. Part longing.

Longing for something she couldn't have.

SUSAN MEIER

No. Something she wouldn't *risk*. Not when financial security was at stake.

She schooled her face. Landing this job didn't merely provide room and board. It secured her future. Attraction was nothing but hormones. She knew firsthand the trouble they could cause.

So, no thanks.

"Nannies always do what's best for the child. Including sanctioning their grandparents."

He sniffed a laugh. "It still sounds perfect to me."

"Your little boy will be my responsibility. I don't take that lightly. I also don't let people push me around."

She'd had enough of that to last a lifetime. Running scared. Changing high schools. Using her mom's maiden name—

She stopped her thoughts. She knew her mind kept jerking in the direction of her secret because of the building. The memories it evoked.

She put herself back into interview mode and said, "I can handle anything your new father dishes out."

Danny laughed. Really laughed. For the first time in months, he felt a little bit of the burden that had become his life chip away. Not only did he have full custody of his son, but he was in the process of hiring a nanny who would make their time together a fun experience.

The last woman he'd interviewed had looked so much like Mary Poppins, he'd almost hired her on the spot, especially considering she had a great résumé. To be fair to the other candidates, he hadn't. But the choice was a no-brainer. He was selecting the nanny who knew how to care for his child, so he wouldn't have even one worry. He could simply enjoy raising his son.

Now this woman—Marnie Olsen—was showing him she could do the job too. Despite being so young.

He looked across the desk at her. Average height. Average weight. In an average floral print dress, blazer and black shoes. Her red-brown hair had been pinned into a knot of some sort at her nape. But she couldn't hide or tone down her lush lips, or the vivid green eyes that watched him carefully.

As they should. If she became Rex's nanny, she'd be knee-deep in Hintonville. The crazy world that had taken over his life. Because of Mark, he'd discovered his son, had two half sisters and was about to get a new stepmom when his dad finally married the love of his life.

But also because of his dad, his adoptive parents felt out of place. Though Danny was trying to smooth things over, he was angry with them for never telling him he was adopted, not warning him that he was the child of a crazy billionaire. Or that someday his life could implode.

In case Mary Poppins didn't take the assignment, he had to interview Marnie Olsen as if she would be entering that messed-up chaotic world.

"The agency sent you to me because they believe you are one of three people qualified to do this job."

"Yes. They told me." She smiled. "Typically, though, I just get assignments. I don't go on interviews."

"This is a long-term thing. My son's mother is about to become a vice president for a bank in Europe. It's a huge opportunity for her and we decided that I was the better candidate to have custody of Rex."

"Mrs. Harper said the assignment could turn permanent."

"Is that a problem?"

"No. I've just never worked with the same child for a year, let alone long term." Her lips lifted into a beautiful smile. "I love children. I'm fully capable of stepping back when an assignment is over…but it would be wonderful to help raise a little boy, watch him grow and learn."

Danny's heart took a funny leap. She was gorgeous when she smiled and her green eyes lit up. He knew instinctively that Rex would love her and, truth be told, if Danny had to have another person living in his home it would be nice to have someone so pleasant.

Mary Poppins slipped a bit on the desirability scale.

He cleared his throat. "Tell me a little bit about yourself."

Something flickered across her face. "Myself?"

Confused by her hesitancy, Danny sat forward. "Your past assignments."

Her smile returned. "I put myself through university as a part-time nanny. It was good money and I could refuse assignments when I needed to study for midterms or finals or do a paper." She shrugged. "I've been with all kinds of kids. I've nannied babies and toddlers and children I took to school." She paused for a second. "Never had a teenager though."

"But you have handled toddlers?"

"The terrible twos are nothing to me."

"Terrible twos are scaring me silly," Danny

said, wincing. "So far Rex has been a perfect angel. But I know trouble is coming."

"Trouble is in the eye of the beholder. All kids can be naughty. All kids experiment. The real bottom line is how *you* react. For instance, if your little boy unravels all the toilet paper, and you explain to him that you know how much fun it is to spin the whole roll to the floor, but that's wasteful, then he learns something. But if you find him in the bathroom surrounded by white tissue, and you go ballistic, you only confuse him."

Considering how Mark had upset everyone's life, he really liked the idea of his son being raised in a quiet, gentle environment. "I get that. My mom was a learn-your-lesson disciplinarian. My dad was a yeller. I learned so much more from my mom."

"Precisely."

"So, what's your favorite part about being a nanny?"

"The kids. I like to get down on the floor and play. I love when they're talkative because they have such an interesting perspective on life. Everything's new to them."

"Rex would love that."

"It's fun for me too. I have been known to create some really great finger paintings."

He laughed.

"And my mom still puts them on the fridge when I bring them home."

"You sound like someone who should be a teacher."

Her face glowed but she sniffed. "No. I love working one-on-one with the kids I'm nannying. I've been studying the latest research on things like the effect of art in a child's life. Music, painting, sculpture, dance…" She nodded at Oswald. "Even pets. The close relationship of a caregiver gives me the chance to expose a child to all those things and watch him or her grow."

That was *exactly* what he wanted for Rex. With all the money in the world at their disposal, his son could be, have or do anything he wanted. Having someone who would expose him to art, teach him to look around and enjoy, would be amazing.

He fought the urge to change his mind about hiring Mary Poppins, a nice, middle-aged woman who'd raised five kids. Marnie was young and happy. He wasn't saying Mary Poppins had a face like a prune… But there was a certain resemblance. His entire life his son would have anything he wanted. Rex needed someone to teach him to appreciate it.

Danny leaned back, angling his elbow on the arm of his chair and resting his jaw on his closed fist. "I'm doing second interviews…with Rex at my penthouse tonight." He hadn't planned on asking Marnie to come to his penthouse, but something in his gut told him she was the one. It had to be wrong. Mary Poppins had the best résumé. Still…

He didn't remember his instincts ever being this strong.

"I was planning on having all the candidates come to my house tonight." He shook his head, hoping the instinct would go away. It didn't. If anything, it got stronger. Plus, he was working with a service. Not one-on-one with the nannies. If Marnie didn't pan out, he could call her boss and exchange her for Mary Poppins.

"But I don't think there's a need for that. I'd like to hire you."

Her mouth fell open. She gaped at him for a few seconds before she said, "Oh my gosh! That's wonderful!" She bounced up from her seat. "You won't be sorry!"

He hoped he wouldn't be. He waited for a ping of anxiety or a sense that he'd made a mistake, but nothing came. He wrote down the address, then stood and handed it across the desk. "I'll see you tonight at eight."

Her face absolutely glowed. "See you at eight."

He watched her leave, his gut positive he'd done the right thing. While his brain hoped to hell he wasn't turning into an impulsive goofball like his biological dad.

CHAPTER TWO

As MARNIE SAT in the subway train, everything about that day plowed through her brain. Something good had happened. She'd gotten a job. A fabulous job with income enough that she could save for her real goal: to open her own nanny agency.

But it was with the son of Mark Hinton, crazy billionaire. It hadn't seemed like a big deal when Shirley Harper had given her the job specifics or even in Danny Manelli's office during the interview. But walking through the elegant lobby of his building, familiar fear trickled through her. Danny Manelli might not be crazy, but his biological dad was—

Her past bubbled up unbidden. Secrets. Lies. Bullying. Lots of it done on social media—

Under Marnie Gouse. Not Olsen. It would take some searching to connect the dots.

Plus, most people used a nanny service because they knew the person coming into their home had been vetted. Danny Manelli hadn't said anything about checking her references or looking into her past. He probably trusted the service.

Of course, he trusted the service. That's what rich people did.

When she arrived at the little apartment she shared with her mom, she walked into her bedroom. The laptop on her desk lured her over. She turned it on and immediately looked up Mark Hinton—

And groaned.

There had to be at least eighty articles written about the estate looking for three missing heirs in the time Mark was supposed to have been dead. One particularly troubling article spoke of Danny's half-sister Leni Long. Her phone had been cloned, outing her, when she'd been keeping a low profile.

Danny was right. His situation was crazy… But did that really have anything to do with her? What would the press care about a woman whose job was to change diapers, fix breakfast and lunch?

Maybe nothing.

She knew she was rationalizing because she *wanted* this job. Her entire being rebelled at the idea of giving it up because of one stupid incident when she was young and too trusting—

She licked her dry lips. She hadn't searched her name in years. Even if it turned up empty, all a search did was dredge up memories that filled her with shame.

But today, she ran her hand along the smooth edge of the laptop. Her mother had always said, if you hear a noise when you're alone in the apartment, check it out and when you find it's nothing, you'll feel better.

This wasn't a noise. It was a fear about her secret. All along she'd blamed her queasiness on walking into the Shutto Building. What if the instinct was actually a nudge from the universe that Roger Martin had put those pictures online?

Horror tightened her chest, filled her with dread. Her fingers hit the keyboard, as she searched her old name.

Nothing.

She wanted to feel relief, but pictures didn't have to be associated to a name. Somewhere on the dark web the photos he'd taken when she'd fallen asleep after losing her virginity could be up online.

Or not.

She'd spent the last years believing they'd been destroyed. After he'd tried to sell the pictures at school, she'd raced home, filled with shame, and her mom had called the police. In what seemed like minutes, a squad car had been at the school entrance and two uniformed officers had been in front of the principal's desk.

Roger hadn't actually posted the pictures and had carefully disguised the way he offered them for sale on his social media pages. Ten years ago, deleting the pictures from his phone, in front of the police, had satisfied the authorities.

But the shame of it had followed her around. She was bullied at school because her mom had called the police. Because she'd embarrassed Roger. Demonized him.

In her mind, he was a demon. But no one seemed to care about her.

She couldn't think back to that time without feeling trapped, afraid, mortified.

But ten years had gone by. A search had netted nothing. She needed to be brave. Take this job. Enjoy Danny Manelli's little boy. Save for her future.

She turned off her laptop and headed to the closet to get a duffel bag to pack. Changing her name and changing schools had given back her life. But no one could guarantee that Roger Martin didn't have those pictures on a thumb drive.

Or that they wouldn't surface one day.

Still, the older she got, the less she looked like the naive girl in the pictures, and her name was different. Plus, nobody really cared about a nanny. Any household employee was like the woodwork. Present, serving a purpose, but not really interesting.

She took a breath. Maybe the thing to do would be take the job and observe. See if Danny Manelli's life was crazy enough that a reporter might get curious about his nanny.

Even thinking that made her shake her head.

Nobody cared about maids, doormen and nannies!

She forced herself to forget that Roger Martin had been a jackass. A privileged jock. Who'd smirked at her when the police let him leave with a warning and a male bonding slap on the shoulder.

It was that smirk that haunted her—a chilling reminder that he was in charge.

Danny arrived home a little after seven. He walked over to the sofa in his open-plan living space and picked up his son. "How are you doing?"

The yellow-haired two-year-old dressed in bib overalls and a T-shirt said, "Good."

"He had a great time." Danny's half-sister Charlotte rose from the teal sofa. A tall, slim blonde with big blue eyes, she looked comfortable and almost motherly in jeans and a tank top—odd for a woman who'd been more accustomed to a hard hat and construction trailer before she discovered she was a Hinton heir.

"Jace was here for a while and they played tag." She huffed out a sigh. "That kid can run! I thought Jace and I were in good shape, but Rex ran rings around us."

Rex giggled. Charlotte tickled his tummy. "Oh, you won this afternoon but Uncle Jace and I will be back."

"I really appreciate you and Leni watching him today. Having Alisha bring him this morning was a shock. Apparently, her employer wanted her in Spain right away and she had to leave immediately. I'm just glad I already had the nursery set up and essentials bought for the weekends I had visitation. I don't know what I'd have done without you."

"Hey, that's what family does." She laughed. "Or at least that's what I'm told. How do three people who were raised as only children end up siblings?"

"Our dad was a runaround."

She snorted and picked up her big purse. "That should be my line." She leaned in and kissed Rex's cheek, then Danny's. "I've got to go. Let me know if you need help interviewing nannies."

"Actually, I hired one."

Charlotte stopped halfway to the elevator. "Really?"

"I don't have the luxury of time. Rex is here now, and I need help. I called Jace this morning and he suggested an agency. Said it was the best nanny service in the business. They sent over three good candidates. I liked the one who looked a bit like Mary Poppins, but there was another candidate who seemed like she might be better."

"Better how?"

"She's younger." He shook his head. "I don't know... It seems like she has more energy or something."

Charlotte took a step toward him. "After losing three games of tag, I'd say energy is a big plus."

"Yes. And she's already been vetted by the agency. I don't have to do a background check myself or call references. I know she's reputable."

Charlotte's smile unexpectedly drooped. "You're not checking *anything*?"

"That's the whole purpose of going through an

agency. Especially this one. Jace says they are the best."

Charlotte laughed. "He does know what he's talking about." She frowned. "It looks like you won't need me anymore."

"Don't be disappointed. I'm sure Marnie will have days off, need personal time, take sick days."

"And I can babysit?"

"You and Leni can split the days."

"And there's the drawback to having siblings." She reached out and lightly pinched Rex's cheek. "I don't want to share this little guy."

"Does that mean I can call you at 2:00 a.m. when he starts wailing?"

She breezed toward the elevator again, slinging her big gray purse over her shoulder. "Not a chance. But I am good for afternoons and weekends." She pressed the button. "Tell your nanny that."

The doors opened and Rex and Danny waved goodbye. As the elevator door closed behind his sister, he carried Rex to the kitchen. "I'm sure your aunt Charlotte fed you dinner but let's see about a snack."

Generally, he knew what he was doing, but he didn't remember all the specifics about Rex's routine. He reached for the three single-spaced pages of notes Rex's mom, Alisha, had given Danny when she shifted custody that morning.

"It says here you get a snack."

Rex's eyes widened with pleasure. "Snack."

"Before bed," Danny added, finishing the sentence he'd started.

Rex frowned.

"Maybe some juice to tide you over. We don't want you messy when the new nanny gets here."

"Nanny."

Danny laughed. "You have a really interesting repeating words thing going on. I'm guessing that's part of how you learn."

"Learn."

Danny sniffed and kissed Rex's forehead before going to the refrigerator. He pulled out the bottle of apple juice, but it bumped the gallon of milk and knocked it to the floor. Danny jumped out of the way with a gasp, but he didn't make it. When the gallon hit the shiny white tile, it broke and milk sprayed outward and upward, soaking him and Rex.

"I'll bet handling this isn't on your mother's list."

Rex blinked twice, his little face twisted, and he yelped, then began to sob. He was coated in milk. So was Danny, but Danny's shoes were also soaked. He held one up and it dripped liquid.

"Definitely not on your mother's list."

He stood there for a few seconds, shell-shocked, but more confused. There were so many things that needed to be done at once. Everything from changing his clothes and Rex's clothes to cleaning the floor and cabinets and getting a new gallon of milk as soon as possible because Rex always drank some before bed.

But looking at the mess—milk on the floor, dripping from the doors of the lower cabinets and soaking his clothes—his brain froze.

CHAPTER THREE

MARNIE WALKED INTO the building containing Danny Manelli's penthouse, and her eyes widened, her breath stalled. Not because she recognized the building—thank God. But from awe. This lobby looked more like someone's sleek, sophisticated living room with midcentury modern sofas sitting at an angle to a stacked stone fireplace and a view of workout equipment beyond a wall of glass.

It reminded her of the building she and her mom had lived in with her dad. New and filled with amenities. Not that she thought her dad lived *here*. He lived on the Upper East Side. Or had fourteen years ago.

There was nothing to fear from him.

A doorman sat at a desk tucked discreetly in the corner. Wearing a white golf shirt, he watched her closely. Probably because she looked lost, out of place. In a way, she was. She couldn't see the elevator that was supposed to take her to the penthouse.

"Excuse me." She walked over to the doorman. "I'm Danny Manelli's new nanny."

"Oh." He smiled. "He told me he'd hired a nanny when he arrived home tonight." He glanced at a sheet of paper on his desk. "You must be Marnie Olsen."

"Yes." To prove her legitimacy, she showed him her ID. "But I don't see an elevator to get to the penthouse."

The doorman laughed and came from behind the desk. "This way."

He led her around a corner to what looked like an ordinary wood-paneled wall. He pressed a button that Marnie hadn't even seen, and the wall opened.

She gaped at it, her chest tightening as it began to sink in that this was no ordinary building. But she reminded herself she was here on a scouting mission. If anything went sideways or looked like it might cause someone to check into her past, she could quit. The agency would have someone at Danny Manelli's penthouse an hour after she left.

But she wasn't going to be a wimp about this. This job was phase two of her plan. Phase one had been get her degree. Phase two was save money while she learned everything she could, so she could start her own nanny service. She had to check this out.

Still, taking another glance at the upscale surroundings, a building more elegant than the homes of her usual clients, something inside her brain said, "Run."

She ruthlessly stomped it out. *So Danny Manelli was rich? Maybe even a billionaire?* Lots of them led perfectly normal lives. And the paparazzi didn't stalk them like everyone believed. No one had ever been interested in her dad. Just because someone was wealthy, it didn't mean they were a target. Paparazzi liked the crazy people, the ostentatious, the billionaires who put themselves out on social media doing ridiculous things.

True, Mark Hinton was out-there, but Danny, her actual boss, was a sedate lawyer. Clearly a successful one, but not someone who'd raise the media's eyebrows. Just like all her other employers. A new nanny wouldn't even be a blip on anyone's radar. Plus, she'd searched social media to ensure her name didn't come up.

If tonight and tomorrow went okay, she'd be fine. And firmly in phase two of her plan. Firmly in control of her life.

After the doorman punched in the code, she

stepped into the elevator, and the little car shot off like a rocket.

The ride to the top floor took mere seconds. The door opened and Marnie gaped. The huge open-plan floor space was decorated with ultramodern furniture and displayed a panoramic view of Manhattan through the back wall of glass. It was so spectacular her breath shimmied.

Warning bells went off in her head. The little voice that said, "Run," returned full force. People who lived in places like this weren't normal. Even if they tried to be normal, how could they be? If anyone other than Mark Hinton had been lost at sea, he might have been declared dead, but it wouldn't have made the national news. And the three heirs, finally found, wouldn't have become overnight celebrities.

This job was too risky.

She reached to punch the down button on the elevator, but before her finger hit, the cries of a toddler pierced the air.

A sense of duty stopped her hand midair.

She waited a second, and when the cries continued, she exited the elevator and almost stepped on the puppy.

She dropped the duffel bag containing all her necessities and stooped to brush her hand along his back. "Oh my goodness. Wiggles! You're going to have to learn to be more careful around people's feet."

The dog barked once.

She glanced around again. Except for Rex's cries, the place was eerily quiet. Where was Danny Manelli?

She rose, looking around. "Where is everybody?"

He barked again.

The little boy's sobs got louder as she ventured farther into the penthouse. The white kitchen area had black and gray trellis tiles for a backsplash and marble countertops. A teal toaster and coffeemaker brightened the huge space. But those sort of led the eye to the teal sofa with matching paisley chairs, which sat in front of a baby grand piano that sat in front of the amazing view of Manhattan.

The cries got louder.

"Mr. Manelli?" She eased toward the hall that she assumed led to bedrooms. "Danny?"

Nothing.

Following the sound of the baby's sobs, she made her way down the corridor until she reached the door where they were the loudest. She turned the knob to find the most luxurious nursery she'd ever seen.

Everything was blue, silver and white. Except the crib, which was cherrywood. Beside the crib was a changing table, where Danny wrestled with a two-year-old and a diaper.

She called, "I'm here," as she slid the puppy to the floor and entered the room.

Danny glanced over his shoulder at her. "Hey. Sorry about the chaos. I spilled a gallon of milk."

She winced. "Oh, that's not good." The front of his white shirt was soaked. So were the black trousers he'd had on at the office that day. She might not be taking the job, but this guy needed help. She'd tell him after things were settled.

"Okay. How about this? Let me dress Rex while you take off those wet clothes."

He stepped back. "A milk-soaked shirt *is* uncomfortable."

She laughed and walked to the changing table. "Scoot. I'll handle this. We'll meet in the kitchen."

Danny left the nursery and Marnie glanced down at Rex who had quieted once his dad shifted away. Naked, waiting for a fresh diaper, he blinked tear-filled eyes at her.

"Look at all that pretty yellow hair," she said, passing a hand through the curls. Regret that she wouldn't get to know him drifted through her. "And blue eyes. You are adorable! You don't know me, but your daddy hired me to be your nanny," she said, making short order of the diaper. She wasn't exactly lying. His dad had hired her. She'd simply not be taking the job. But she wouldn't leave a single dad in this much trouble.

She looked at the clock. "It's close to eight," she said, one hand on the baby, the other opening the closet door to find a dresser. "So, I'm thinking of putting you into pajamas." Taking a long reach, she found one-piece pj's in the second drawer. She plucked out a pair and slid the bottoms over his feet and legs.

He stared at her.

Her chest tightened. He was the most beautiful child she'd ever seen. "I must be a real curiosity to you, if you've stopped crying." She slid his arms into the top. "Is there broccoli in my teeth?"

One corner of his mouth kicked up as if he understood.

Her heart swelled. In two minutes with this little boy, she was in love. "I knew you liked me."

"He does seem to." Danny's voice came from behind her and sounded greatly relieved.

Marnie's helper gene flushed with pride. She

couldn't stay, but she wouldn't leave someone who clearly needed her.

If he'd spilled enough milk, he needed her.

She finished pulling the top of the one-piece pajamas over Rex's shoulders and pulled the zipper over his tummy. "I hope you don't mind. I took the liberty of putting him into pajamas. I assume he'll get a snack and then be off to bed."

"Yes." Danny winced. "I had forgotten his bedtime is between eight and eight-thirty when I asked you to come at eight. I should have said seven."

"No biggie," she said cheerfully, as she lifted the little boy from the changing table and settled him on her arm. Once they got Rex into bed, she'd tell Danny she'd changed her mind, remind him that the agency could send over another nanny and be on her way. "We have a half hour or so to get him a snack, brush his teeth and maybe read him a story."

Danny inched nearer. "He likes stories." When he got close, Rex reached for him.

Marnie handed him over. "He also likes you."

Danny planted a kiss on his cheek. "Hard to believe, since I'm not very good with him yet. But he met me a few months ago. We've had lots of visits."

She remembered him telling her that he hadn't even known he was a father. Yet, here he was not merely pitching in, but obviously determined to be a good dad. "Babies have an instinct about people. And they are patient. If he likes you, he'll cut you lots of slack."

Heading out of the nursery, Danny laughed. "He'd better because he's stuck with me."

Marnie followed him out into the hall and back to the open space. Her breath hitched a bit at the luxury of it all. Shiny and expensive, it had clearly been furnished by a decorator. She'd bet her meager savings the abstract paintings on the wall were originals.

"I'm sure he doesn't consider himself stuck with you. He obviously loves you."

"Yeah. We'll see how he feels tomorrow when there's no milk."

They walked into the kitchen area and around the corner of the huge center island, and there stood Wiggles, lapping up the milk that had spilled when the thin plastic container split.

She grabbed him. "Oh, we can't have that!"

"Really? He seems to like it."

"He's been alone out here for a good ten minutes. Lord only knows how much he drank. Plus, some dogs are lactose intolerant." She smiled at

Danny. He looked like sex on a spoon wearing black sweatpants and a big T-shirt. She'd thought he was handsome in a white shirt and tie. In the sweatpants and big T-shirt, he was casual, approachable and so sexy her mouth wanted to water.

"Lactose intolerant?"

"Um. Yes." It took a second to get her bearings. It wasn't like her to react to a good-looking employer. Fathers of toddlers were almost always young and handsome. And she never cared. But her hormones must believe noticing was okay. Since she wasn't keeping the job, it didn't matter how attractive she found him. As soon as everything was cleaned and the baby tucked away, she'd tell him and never see him again.

"But the good news is, you can use this as a test. If Wiggles doesn't have any digestive problems tonight, you can take it as a sign that he can have milk every once in a while."

She surveyed the kitchen until she saw Rex's highchair. "Here's what we'll do. We'll put Rex in his chair with some crackers and a cup of juice. You go to the neighborhood store and get a new gallon of milk while I tackle this mess."

"That's generous, but I didn't hire you to house-clean—"

"No buts. Your son needs milk in the morning, and if we leave this mess too long, trust me, it will smell. This might also be a good time to take the puppy out for his nightly business. I can handle all this while you're gone."

"You're sure?"

For a rich guy, he didn't seem to treat staff with authority. Still, his uncertainty endeared him to her. Mixed with her attraction, it filled her with warmth.

She ignored it. He *was* an extremely handsome guy. His dark eyes were clear and looking into them, she felt like she could see the whole way to his soul. If she thought working for a superrich guy could cause her problems, being attracted to her employer would doubly do so. The press would lap it up the way Wiggles lapped up that milk.

She almost groaned at her thoughts. She wasn't even keeping this job. Stupid to dwell on being attracted to him. Her thoughts had to be running out of control because of proximity. And how sweet he was with his son.

Luckily, he was leaving.

"Yes! I'm fine. Go get the milk."

Danny put a leash on Wiggles, grabbed his wallet from the center island and headed for the door. "You're sure you're okay?"

"Yes!"

"I can send up the doorman."

She laughed. "To do what? Seriously. I'm fine."

In the elevator, Danny let out a long breath. He'd just left his child with a stranger—

A stranger he'd hired as a nanny, who worked for the service used and recommended by his future brother-in-law, Jace MacDonald, owner of one of the premier security companies in the world.

Rex was fine. *Danny* wasn't.

He'd always seen himself as competent. Sure, he and Rex had had a few odd moments the times he'd visited, but Danny had plowed through. Yet spilled milk had frozen him.

Because too many things needed to be done simultaneously. But Marnie Olsen had surveyed the situation, made a plan and got them all going in the right direction.

Setting Oswald on the sidewalk so he could trot along, Danny decided that proved he'd made the right choice in hiring her. No. That was an over-simplification. He hadn't simply made the right choice. Marnie rocked. Smart and strong, with an organized mind and total grasp of what she was doing, she'd easily righted the chaos.

That weird feeling rolled through him again. Part relief that he genuinely believed Marnie Olsen had been the correct choice for nanny, and part warmth.

Delicious warmth. She was personable, competent, easygoing and—

He winced. Pretty. She was so damned pretty.

Plus, thanks to her yoga pants and pink T-shirt, he also knew she had a smoking hot body.

Which was irrelevant. His world was in turmoil and he wasn't an idiot. He needed someone strong and smart who could handle his crazy life, much more than he needed or even *wanted* a romance. A woman he'd been intimate with had had his child and never told him. He'd only found out a few months ago. His ability to trust would need time to regroup. Romance was the furthest thing from his mind.

And Marnie Olsen was *the nanny he needed.* His gut had not been wrong when he hired her. He wouldn't screw that up by indulging an attraction.

He and Oswald took a side trip to the park for the pup to do his business, then they meandered the few blocks to a small deli, bought milk and headed home. He wouldn't let himself think about how pretty Marnie was anymore. All that was beside the point. He needed a competent nanny.

Arriving at his penthouse, he found her in the kitchen, sitting on a stool beside the highchair, making his son laugh. The milk had been cleaned up. Rex polished off the last of the juice in his sippy cup.

Calm settled over him. The gut instinct returned. He wanted this calm, *needed* this calm.

He'd absolutely made the right choice.

"I don't know what I would have done without your help." The puppy pranced as far as his leash would allow him, then sat, his chest out, his head regal, and stared at Marnie as if showing her he could be a good boy. "I can't thank you enough. You have no idea how happy I am you took this job."

Guilt stricken, Marnie looked over at Danny Manelli as he unfastened Wiggles's leash. The dog immediately raced to her, and she picked him up so he could lick her cheeks. Rex giggled with glee.

Oh Lord. Did he have to be so nice?

His son so adorable.

His puppy so sweet?

Plus, this place might be elegant, but Danny and his son were very normal. The *job* was normal. Add to that that she liked phase two of her plan and the idea of socking away tons of cash so that by the time Rex outgrew her services, she'd have plenty to start her own business.

"As soon as we have Rex settled, I can show you to your quarters." He pointed to the right. "Your room is back there, next to the guest bath and a laundry area and across from the family room."

She debated, but all her doubts and fears seemed tiny compared to how much this little family needed her—

How much she wanted this job—

She cleared her throat.

Don't quit. Be brave. Take the next step. Don't lose this opportunity over something that's probably buried.

She took a slow, strong breath. "Thanks. If you don't mind, I'll unpack and acclimate a bit tonight so I can handle everything in the morning."

"Tomorrow's Saturday and I don't have to go to work. We can run over the important stuff then. Tonight, we'll tackle the musts. Like, I know you're probably wondering why your quarters are so far from the nursery, but the baby monitoring system is elaborate and effective." He laughed. "You'll know when he cries."

She smiled. "Great. I'm familiar with most monitoring systems."

"Good."

There. See? Easy peasy.

Nothing was going to go wrong. Nothing was going to happen. No boogeyman would jump out of a bush and realize who she was.

She was nobody.

And Danny Manelli was just a rich guy, a simple lawyer. Sure, his dad was out there, but she hadn't seen his name in the papers in at least a month. No one would care to poke around in the life of his son's nanny. And even if they did, she hadn't found anything in her search.

She was fine.

Danny Manelli needed her. *Rex* needed her.

And she wanted phase two of her life. If anything *ever* looked like it was going sideways, she could call Shirley at the agency and go back home and be nobody again.

But if things worked out, she'd live in a beautiful home, raise a beautiful little boy and put away enough cash to start over.

She'd never thought of leaving New York, but what if she took her money and went to another city? A place where no one knew her? A place where the chances of running into Roger Martin were so slim, she'd be free?

She suddenly realized that was her goal. Not merely starting her own agency but doing it in another city.

Chicago. Tampa. Dallas.

The possibilities were endless and along with them came freedom. Real freedom.

But to do that she'd need money. And this job provided plenty of it.

CHAPTER FOUR

ONCE REX WAS SETTLED, Danny showed Marnie her quarters, a suite with a sitting room with a big screen television, a bedroom and bathroom. The color scheme revolved around soft sage mixed with cream and gray in the bathroom and bedroom with a darker sage and gray in the sitting room. Rustic hardwood floors with gray and white area rugs pulled it all together.

She could have spun around with her arms outstretched, taking it all in, but she simply smiled and told Danny it was lovely.

Pleased, he'd nodded. "I want to run through a few more things, then you can unpack, watch TV, do whatever you like."

"Great."

He led her out to the huge open area. As they passed the center island that separated the kitchen from the rest of the space, he grabbed some papers from the marble countertop.

"These are instructions Rex's mom wrote for us. They don't merely set out his routine—Alisha also mentioned a lot of his likes and dislikes." He handed them to her, then sat on one of the paisley chairs.

Lowering herself to the sofa, she scanned them, then glanced up. "This is wonderful, very thorough."

"Rex's mom is one of those overorganized people. She thinks of everything."

"That'll be a big help."

"I know you're probably confused about the arrangement with Rex's mom, so let me just say that she and I had a very short-term relationship. She got pregnant but didn't tell me. My biological dad, who I recently discovered had been monitoring my life, uncovered Rex. In order to tell me about my son, he had to out himself as my father. Anyway, I contacted Alisha, and she and I had been working on visitation when she got a fabulous job opportunity in Spain."

"Spain. Wow."

"I know. She couldn't pass it up. But she also didn't want to take Rex away from everyone. Her parents and two sisters live in Manhattan. I live here. In Spain, Rex would only have her. After some soul-searching, she decided to let me raise Rex. The job in Spain is her dream job, but it comes with tons of responsibility and she'll be working a lot. In the end, she realized it would be better for Rex to be around people who love him. She'll get him for a week or two every summer and one holiday a year. And, of course, she'll come to New York a few times a year to see him."

"That's wonderful for you."

"Yes. It was hard coming to terms with the fact that Alishia hadn't intended to tell me about Rex. But once Mark's private investigators found out about the baby, she was generous. She didn't hedge. She let me see him. A lot. When this job offer came up, she didn't take only herself into consideration, she thought of what was best for Rex. Now here I am, a real father."

He smiled and attraction hit her again. His sweats and oversize T-shirt made him look sexy, especially with his short black hair slightly untidy, his smile quick and genuine. Connection wove through her. The kind of feeling she'd always believed a person would have when they clicked with someone romantically. When they imagined a future with them—

She redirected it. The connection was a result of him being a nice guy, someone who wanted to be a good father. Every nanny in the world could appreciate that. That's why they clicked. As for the future? She wanted to be Rex's nanny for a long time. *That's* what she'd focus on.

"I'm glad everything worked out."

"I am too." He rose from his chair. "Okay. That's it. With Rex in bed, the rest of the evening is yours."

She nodded. "Thanks." She walked to her room, through the sitting room and to the bedroom where her duffel bag lay on the soft sage-colored spread. She took a long breath, as the joy of getting this job hit her fully. She had a gorgeous little boy to care for, a luxurious suite all to herself and would earn enough money that her goal was on track.

And maybe, after all these years, so was her life? For the first time in a decade she hadn't let her fear rule her decision. The sense of taking back her life rolled through her, along with a weird something—

Oh good grief, she felt normal.

Normal.

Who'd have thought experiencing what every other person in the world felt every day would be so empowering, so welcome, so joyous?

Saturday morning, as Marnie finished helping Rex with breakfast, Danny grabbed Wiggles's leash.

Drying her hands in a paper towel, she said, "Are you taking him for his walk?"

Danny laughed. "I'm surprised he waited this long."

Now that she'd acclimated, she'd decided to treat this like any other job. Do all the things she did with the upwardly mobile executives she'd worked for over the years.

"What do you say Rex and I go with you?"

His dark eyes lit. "Go with me?"

"I'd like to get an idea of where Wiggles goes on his walk, and the lay of the land in the neighborhood."

"That makes sense."

He might be clueless about some childcare issues, but he was open-minded. Another thing that would make working for him easy. "Do you have a stroller?"

"A big fancy one and a little thing my mom called an umbrella stroller."

"Let's take the big fancy one."

They loaded Rex in the stroller, leashed Wiggles and rode the elevator to the lobby. Danny pushed the stroller through the revolving door. Marnie followed him out into the almost empty street, typical of early Saturday morning on Park

Avenue. The scents of warm pastries and coffee hit her immediately. Her stomach growled.

"We'll pick up something from the bakery down the block when we get back."

She grimaced. "Sorry about that. My stomach usually doesn't growl, but I inadvertently skipped dinner last night."

"You should have said something! There's a whole fridge full of food."

"I seriously forgot." She'd been too busy being confused, then bold, then overwhelmed with how wonderful it was to take what felt like the next step in her life. "But I'm going to hold you to a visit to that bakery."

They strolled down the quiet street. Trees lined the sidewalk in front of buildings that rose to the blue sky. "This is beautiful."

Danny glanced around. "I like it. I didn't think I would, but once I moved in it felt like home."

"I can see why." The area had the mood of a city, but there was a sophisticated hominess about it. The few people milling about wore jeans and T-shirts or yoga pants and tank tops. Sun sneaking through the thick leaves of the trees almost made it look enchanted.

Wiggles found a comfortable tree and did his

business. Marnie gave Danny the leash and she took the stroller.

After handling things, Danny said, "And this is about as far as we get every morning."

"We should walk another block or two. Give Rex some outside time."

"You can take him to the park this afternoon after his nap."

She looked around, comfortable with her surroundings and positive she could find her way. "Good idea."

As the words popped out of her mouth, she saw a tall, slim man approaching. Even from a distance she knew who he was. Her stomach knotted. He read a newspaper as he walked, his gait unmistakable.

She stopped. Danny stopped. "What?"

Her dad.

All this time she'd been so worried about Roger that she'd only given a passing thought to her dad because he lived on the Upper East Side. *Not here.*

He walked right by her. She could think he was preoccupied with his newspaper but the truth was, even if he'd looked her in the face, he wouldn't have recognized her. She'd been twelve the last time he'd seen her. He didn't know her as an adult.

Sadness billowed from her stomach to her chest.

"Marnie?"

She shook her head to clear it. This was a plum assignment and she was very lucky to have it. Like it or not, her dad was a wealthy guy. She shouldn't be surprised he'd moved to Park Avenue, probably to a new, fancier building. She'd gotten over his loss years ago. Seeing him had just thrown her, that's all.

Her old fears returned. If she could so easily run into her father, was she tempting fate with Roger Martin? His family was in the same tax bracket as her dad, as Danny Manelli.

Her past came tumbling back. Her father leaving her mother. Being broke after being accustomed to being wealthy. Getting kicked out of their apartment. The lack of stability.

And the man responsible was walking down the same street she'd be using every day.

Had it been a mistake to take this job?

No!

There was no way to get beyond her stupid past but to move forward, to be courageous, to enter this world and put all that behind her. Particularly given that this job provided the stability and security she hadn't had since she was twelve.

She took a breath, knowing acknowledgment was the first step to shattering the hold her past had over her. "It's okay. I just saw someone I knew."

He peered up the street and then down again. "Someone you knew?"

Face it. Look the past in the eye and steal its power.

"Actually, it was my dad."

He frowned. "Your *dad*?" He glanced around again. "I didn't hear anyone say hello. You didn't stop—"

She batted a hand. The best way to regain control was to minimize what had happened. Think of it as unimportant. A blip. "It's nothing." She turned the stroller toward Danny's building. "He... Well, I'm sure he didn't recognize me. He hasn't seen me since I was twelve. He took my brother and left me and my mom."

Danny stared at her, so confused he sputtered, "He left your mom, and you haven't seen him since?"

"Yes," Marnie said, as if she were giving a report in a boardroom. Calm. In control. "I found his condo and tried to visit when I was fourteen. I wanted to let him know my mom was fine and that we should…you know…visit or something, but he wouldn't see me. Wouldn't let me see my brother either. He had a maid tell me to leave." She gazed around, as if seeing the whole street with a different perspective. "He must have moved again…to Park Avenue. I know he wouldn't walk more than a block for the paper."

Sympathy washed through Danny. "I'm sorry."

She shrugged. "Don't be. Lots of time has gone by. I'm accustomed to it now." She smiled brightly. Too brightly. "It's no biggie."

"It would have been a biggie to me."

"It was. In the beginning." She bit her lip, then her demeanor brightened again. "But, you know, life goes on."

"Still, a father who didn't want to see you? That's awful." He sniffed. "Look at what I'm saying. I literally found out a few months ago that I had a biological father. I went through a phase where I was almost incapacitated by the realization that, no matter how much he was edging into my life now, he hadn't wanted me when I was born. Or he wouldn't have had my biological mother give me up for adoption." He sniffed again. "He kept saying he'd wanted me. That he'd hidden my two sisters and me for our safety. But…" He shrugged. "Actions speak louder than words."

"My dad's a selfish, self-centered perfectionist."

"That's my dad too." He shook his head. "I don't want to be like him."

She smiled. "Good plan."

She rolled the stroller up to the penthouse's building, but Danny stopped her.

She gave him a confused look.

"We're going to the bakery for bagels, remember?"

"That's right." She shook her head, embarrassed that she'd forgotten, then she winced. "I was kind of hoping for a Danish."

He laughed. "Whatever you want."

They ambled into the nearby bakery, and she examined the pastries as if she were choosing a diamond. He almost told her to pick two, but something stopped him. If her dad lived on Park Avenue, he had to be wealthy. Yet, here she was, a nanny, because her father had left her and her mother.

Their lives were flipped.

She'd started off the child of a wealthy man and had become lower middle class. He'd started off the child of a lower middle-class blue-collar couple and was suddenly wealthy.

And he was complaining?

Guilt surged through him, but an unexpected suspicion tiptoed in on its heels. Was it odd that she'd admitted something so personal to someone she barely knew? As a lawyer, he was accustomed to people telling him their troubles. But he wasn't her lawyer. He was her boss.

Jace, as administrator of the Hinton security team, and his two half sisters who were living his nightmare had warned him that now that he was heir to one of the world's biggest fortunes, people would scam him. Work to get close to him, tell him sad stories and hope he opened the purse strings.

The thought was so shocking he shook his head to clear it. Marnie was a good person. He could feel it in his bones. And her life had been hard. She wouldn't lie about that.

Watching her so carefully choose a simple Danish confirmed that. Having had to scrape for money, he knew pride when he saw it. The fierce need to never overstep boundaries. Never exploit a kindness for fear of looking greedy.

He wouldn't buy her two Danish. She wouldn't

eat the second one. He would buy the one she selected. And not make her feel uncomfortable.

They returned to the penthouse. Wiggles raced inside, and Danny had to wrestle the exuberant pup to remove his leash. "I think it's time to talk about obedience school."

"I have a whole list saved on my laptop. I can print it out for you or send it to your phone."

"Send it to my phone."

"Okay." Marnie sat Rex in the highchair and gave him a sippy cup of milk before she headed for the one-cup coffeemaker. "Do you want coffee with your bagel?"

"Yes. But I'll get it. You're not a maid, remember?"

She smiled sheepishly. "No. But there's no reason we can't be friends. We are living together. We'll be in each other's hair a lot. Might as well work together."

His suspicions about her crept up on him again. But he squelched them. They were living together. Being kind just made sense. Particularly since she was the first person in months with whom he felt comfortable talking. Maybe because her life was as messed up as his?

"I don't mind making coffee for my friend."

He forced the suspicion away. "Okay. A cup of regular, please."

Wiggles barked. Danny walked to the counter. "I give him a treat when we get back from our walk."

He pulled a biscuit from a cookie jar in the corner. The dog grabbed it and raced away.

Marnie's eyes widened. "Good thing I didn't look in there. I might have thought they were cookies and eaten one."

Danny laughed, back to feeling good about hiring her. Not just because she was a great nanny, but because she deserved a break. After a few minutes of making coffee and finding cream, they sat at the counter, her with her Danish. Him with a bagel slathered in thick cream cheese.

She took a bite, squeezed her eyes shut and groaned. "Oh man! This is *sooo* good."

"Best bakery in the area," he replied, but he watched her. The clicks of rightness he kept getting with her had probably been his subconscious picking up on the similarities in their lives.

"We seem to have a lot in common."

She peeked over at him. "Oh yeah? Like what?"

He ignored the lightning bolt of attraction that shot through him when their gazes connected. Not only was it a cliché to have a thing for the nanny, but it seemed like she needed a friend as much as he did.

"We both understand being lower middle class."

She glanced around his penthouse. "Looks like you've moved up in the world."

"But I won't forget my roots. I don't want to."

"I get that. I didn't really want to forget my dad, either, but he made his choices."

"And my biological dad made his."

She pulled a small bite off her Danish. "You're the first person I've told about my dad."

He could have drowned in her soft green eyes and almost did drown in the sense of rightness that filled him. Not just that he could tell her almost anything, but more.

More?

Now that the attraction had coupled with a real connection, what he felt for her grew and edged in the direction of something with relationship potential. But he didn't want to be a cliché. And he sure as hell didn't intend to drag her into something she didn't want.

And *he* didn't want.

Did he?

No. A woman with whom he'd had a one-night stand had had his child and not told him. His parents had hidden the fact that he was adopted. His biological dad kept saying he loved all his kids, but he'd lived decades without making contact with any of them.

The problem wasn't that Marnie was his employee. It was trust. Right now, Danny's trust issues had trust issues. That's why he kept getting weird suspicions about her. He couldn't look at a situation normally. He couldn't look at a person without wondering what they were hiding.

She was a good person with a hard life just trying to make a living, and his thoughts had jumped to a very bad place over her telling him a simple truth about her life.

So, no. Even considering a relationship right now was out of the question. No matter how beautiful she was or how soft she looked or how happy he was when she was around—

He jumped off his stool. What the hell was he thinking! He had to stop letting his thoughts go crazy when she was around. "It's time for me and Rex to video call my mom and dad."

"The ones from upstate?"

Her question was normal. Easily spoken. Like a conversation between employer and nanny. She hadn't noticed him mooning over her. This had to be the end of thinking things like wanting more. He didn't want more. He had enough on his plate with a child to raise, a new dad and coworkers who didn't know how to deal with him now that he was superrich.

He strolled over to Rex in the highchair. "Yes. Video calling is a good way to stay in touch."

The smile she gave him sent goose bumps shivering down his arms. Which was nuts. He barely knew her. Plus, he had a million reasons his reactions were wrong. That's why he was taking Rex and leaving her to herself. The woman had had enough trouble in her life. She didn't need her boss developing a crush on her.

He took Rex out of the highchair and headed for his room, confusion making him shake his head. The problem was what he felt for her wasn't a crush. It was a connection. If it was a crush or a simple sexual attraction, he could squelch either one of those. The connection filled him with longing for something important, something real.

But he wasn't in a place for any of this. After everything that had happened to him, he might never trust again. If Marnie was as good a person as he thought, she deserved better.

CHAPTER FIVE

HE KEPT HIMSELF and Rex busy for the rest of the morning, letting Marnie continue to settle in. She helped with Rex's lunch, then they took the little boy to the nursery for his nap. Danny stepped back so Marnie could change him. It wasn't that he didn't want to do diaper duty. He was still monitoring Rex's reactions to her. She might seem perfect, but they were in a probationary period. He couldn't forget that. He had to get his head in the game.

The little boy giggled as she chatted with him while removing one diaper and putting on another. Danny's heart lifted. Diaper change complete, she picked up Rex and cuddled him. Danny's son returned her cuddle, snuggling against her neck and shoulder. She and his son were a good match. And *that's* what mattered.

Not some nebulous feeling that kept nudging him to want things with her that weren't appropriate.

His phone rang. Glad for the distraction, he

pulled it from his pocket and groaned when he saw the name on the screen. "I have to take this."

"That's fine. I'll put him down for his nap."

Danny said, "Great. Thanks."

Closing the door behind him, he stepped into the hall feeling better. He had no idea why he felt a connection with her except that both of their lives had been weird. He'd never had a nanny before, so sure—maybe he'd let himself go overboard with the chitchat. But he could end that. She was too good with his son for him to ruin it because his thoughts veered off in the wrong direction.

And just in case those crazy suspicions that tiptoed into his brain were valid, not giving in to his attraction would protect him.

He finished his call. When he found her in the kitchen, sitting at the center island, reading Alisha's notes, he said, "I've never employed a nanny before, so I'm not sure how this works. Do we eat lunch together?"

She glanced up and smiled. "Sometimes, I guess. If we have things to discuss." As he walked into the kitchen area, she said, "In my other assignments, most days I'd grab a sandwich and take it to my room to study. But I got my degree in May."

"Shirley mentioned that you'd just graduated."

"It took a boatload of years, because I couldn't afford to take a full course load most semesters. Anyway, that's over. Now I move on to phase two of my career path."

"Phase two?" He looked at her. "I did say I hoped this situation would turn permanent, right?"

She batted a hand. "I won't be leaving you. My plan is to start my own nanny service, but that's at least a decade down the road. Maybe two." She bit her lower lip. "Honestly, the money you're paying will go a long way to help me reach my dream."

After tossing a loaf of bread to the counter, he opened the refrigerator door saying, "Ham or turkey?"

"I should say turkey, but I'm in the mood for ham. Mustard too, if you've got it."

"I have everything." He brought the deli meats to the island, feeling better. They were alone and holding a normal conversation. No weird attraction. No noticing odd things about her. No suspicions.

"Tell me about the business you want to start."

"It's going to be a lot like Shirley's, but I plan to cater to people who want their kids to get a certain experience. I'm starting to map out ways to get music and art into kids' daily routines."

"That's right. You did mention something about that."

"As Rex gets older, he'll be exposed to a lot of it."

"That's great!" He handed her the plate holding the sandwich he'd made for her. "You think you need to work for me a decade or so to save sufficient cash to get started?"

She nodded.

"Why don't you borrow some money, or better yet, look for investors?"

She rolled her eyes. "Seriously? You know someone who wants to invest in a nanny service?"

"You'd be surprised what people will invest in."

"No one I know."

He slid the plate containing his sandwich to the other side of the island, walked around it and sat on the stool beside her. "Who do you know?"

"That's just it. No one."

"Hey, you now work for a fairly well-connected guy. I won't exactly put out feelers but if someone mentions looking for an investment, I can give your name."

Her face flushed. "That's kind of you, but I

think I need the years I'll be spending with your son to hone my idea."

He could see he'd embarrassed her and remembered how she'd been dumbstruck when she'd seen her dad and even how she'd eagerly chosen her Danish. He backed off. He might have confessed his entire messed up life to her, but he only knew bits and pieces of hers.

For a second that struck him as odd. Lopsided. For as much as it had confused him when she'd told him about her dad, she knew a lot more about him than he knew about her. He fought not to shake his head over his craziness. He got suspicious when she told him about herself, and now he was worried that she knew more about him than he knew about her?

He shrugged off those concerns. He had to stop imagining things that weren't there. "Okay."

"Thanks."

"But just for the heck of it, start looking at the people around you. You could even make note of who comes and goes in *my* life. You never know when a good investor will pop up."

"I will." She picked up the plate holding her sandwich. "I think I'll go to my room. Maybe call my mom."

She didn't look angry or embarrassed, so he

forced himself to interpret her retreat as simply a desire to touch base with her mom.

He said, "Sure," but as she walked down the hall, he called, "Research business plans. That'd be a great way to see what you need to have to entice investors."

She called back, "I'm not ready for that yet."

But there was a laugh in her voice. He really didn't want her to quit the job he'd only given her the day before, but finding investors sometimes took years. Plus, having something impersonal to talk about worked to keep things simple between them, like two friends conversing. If nothing else, thinking of her as a friend was a good idea.

A normal way to treat her.

Neutral.

He didn't want his Hinton Heir suspicions to cause him to lose a very good nanny, a woman who deserved a good job, a woman who was clearly working hard to make a better life for herself.

After Rex finished his nap, they gave him a snack and played with him for a few hours before feeding him dinner, playing again and then getting him ready for bed. Once he was in his crib with the monitor on and the sound machine spreading the soft patter of rain through the room, Danny watched TV in the great room and Marnie retreated to her suite.

Sunday went by in pretty much the same way. Monday, he left her alone with Rex while he went to work. Twice, he video called to check on them. Both times he felt like an idiot. Rex giggled and clung to her. He even kissed her cheek once.

The first week went by in a gloriously simple fashion. No drama. No more spilled milk. Suspicions gone, he made easy conversation with Marnie over dinner that he had delivered. There was no trauma at bedtime. There were no visits from Mark, who was busy planning his wedding with his fiancée, Penny, Charlotte's mother. And, finally comfortable, Rex slept through the night.

Marnie took the following Sunday off to visit her mother, sleeping at her mom's apartment and was back—cheerful and happy—on Monday morning at a quarter to eight.

His work life improved. As if the excitement of discovering their coworker was a billionaire had lost its luster, lawyers, investigators, secretaries, assistants and paralegals all returned to treating him like just another lawyer.

The next Saturday, Danny woke feeling fantastic. Through the monitor by his bed, he heard the happy sounds of Marnie dressing Rex for the day and Rex's giggles. Peace and joy filled him, and he bounced out of bed, heading for the shower.

His world was back in order, and he got to spend the entire day with his two favorite people in the world, his son and his son's nanny.

He didn't let himself dwell on the comment that had raced through his brain as he slid into jeans and a T-shirt and ambled into the kitchen, where Marnie fed Rex. He'd settled his attraction by acknowledging she was gorgeous and easy to talk to and shifting his attention to being her friend. She needed help. He was in a position where he could help. That was their connection.

Walking into the kitchen area, he said, "Hey! How is everybody today?"

He bent and kissed Rex's forehead, and the little boy said, "Dad!"

Nothing rivaled the fierce love that surged at the sound of his son calling him Dad. And nothing could ruin this day. Danny wouldn't let it.

The doorman arrived, mail in hand. Danny offered him a cup of coffee, but he refused it, saying good morning to Marnie and retreating to the elevator.

"He seems like a very nice guy."

"He is," Danny said, making himself a cup of

coffee. "He's like you. He has a business that he's organizing. It's kind of a cross between doormen and security guards." He rifled through the mail. "I put him in touch with my half-sister Charlotte's fiancé. They're working on something together now."

She laughed. "Is that what rich people do? Look for business opportunities in every person they meet?"

"So far, I haven't been the one to invest." He paused, pondering that, realizing that he'd never offered her money. He'd squelched his suspicions about her worming her way into his life to get part of the Hinton fortune, so that could only mean he'd taken her caution that she wasn't ready to heart. A very *normal* thing to do. His instincts about her seemed to finally be back on track.

"It's more like I remember myself when I was scrambling to find my place. I identify with people trying to make a move, so I notice things, connect things, put people together."

"That's very nice of you."

He flipped through the mail. "Not really." He wasn't nice. This was him as he normally was. No more freaky suspicions or overwhelming attractions. Just him, living his life.

He got to a fancy envelope, something made

of high-quality paper, clearly an invitation. His old address had been scratched out and his new address written over it.

He opened the envelope and discovered an invitation to a gallery event, featuring the work of Sally McMillen. "This is tonight."

She glanced over. "So?"

"It needs an RSVP and I missed the date. I guess I could still go if I called the coordinator and explained my invitation had been sent to the wrong address, so my RSVP is late."

"You guess you could go? It sounds like so much fun!" She laughed. "It's not like you have to worry about a babysitter."

He peered over at her. "Or maybe I do. This is exactly the kind of thing you should go to, to meet potential investors. It's sponsored by the McCallan family."

She sucked in a breath. "I've heard of them."

"Everybody's heard of them. And anybody who is anybody will be there."

She put her hand on her chest. "And you think *I* should go?"

"Sure? Not to ask for investment money, but just to mingle. Let me introduce you around."

Her face scrunched. "As your nanny?"

"You are starting a nanny business."

"In ten years…"

"Whenever. If you go to one or two of these kinds of things a year, eventually the big players will start remembering your name. Then when you need money, their pocketbooks will already be loosened."

She snorted. "You're nuts."

"I'm serious. We don't have to stay forever. Just a couple minutes. An hour tops." He frowned. "Is it so horrible to be seen in public with me?"

She said, "No," but she said it too quickly and there was a squeak in her voice. Warmth fluttered through her and she had to hold back a groan. It was not horrible to be seen in public with him. The idea was too appealing.

"Come on. You need a break and it won't hurt to schmooze the players. Plus, my sister Charlotte loves to babysit. She called yesterday to say I should fire you because she hasn't gotten to babysit Rex since I hired you."

She laughed. His half-sisters had visited during Marnie's first week of employment, and while Leni was sweet and kind, Charlotte was a hoot. Plus, she'd comfortably settled into being Rex's nanny, and her life had become wonderful. She didn't want to ruin that by saying or doing something wrong. Especially at a fancy gallery opening.

"Please… This way I don't have to go alone."

She heard a note of something in his voice that reminded her of her first days of working for him. He'd been lost and befuddled but determined to be a good dad. Every day he got a little smarter in his ability to care for Rex. Every day he seemed happier. It might not be her job to keep her boss happy, but the human being in her related to feeling a beat out of step with the rest of the world and wishing for a friend.

"Okay." Her decision had nothing to do with thinking he was adorable. He was a fabulous employer and a good person, and considering how much he tried to help her, she kind of owed him. She didn't have anything to wear, but she had some money saved.

"I'll need a few hours this afternoon to get a dress."

He slid his cell phone from his pocket. "I'll call Charlotte."

She bought a simple black dress, something she could wear again and again, something that would help her blend in. A subway ride took her to her mom's apartment, where she borrowed a string of pearls with teardrop earrings—a set her dad had bought as an anniversary gift. One of the few things her mom hadn't sold for rent money before she finally got child support from Marnie's dad.

The reminder of her dad abandoning her mom filled her with trepidation, but she ignored it. Danny, adopted by middle class parents, was nothing like her father. Plus, this wasn't a date. It was an employer helping his employee.

And the people she would meet? She would see them as investors. She wouldn't fear them. She refused to fear them.

But what if she saw Roger Martin?

Her heart stuttered. Despite running into her dad, two weeks of happily living on Park Avenue, taking Rex and Wiggles for walks, and going to the bakery had shown her that Manhattan might be a small world, but she hadn't seen Roger in it. She'd become settled. Almost confident. She didn't want to lose that over the fear of seeing someone who could have moved out of the city. Hell, he could have moved to Europe. She couldn't be afraid of what *might* happen.

Charlotte arrived around seven to give Rex a chance to get accustomed to her, and Marnie went to her room to dress. Ready by eight and knowing they needed to leave soon to get to the gallery, she walked into the open area, snapping closed the clasp of her black clutch bag after stashing her ID and cell phone.

She glanced up to see Charlotte's lips curve into an odd smile and Danny's mouth fall open.

"Wow."

"You can say that again," Charlotte sing-songed. "You look amazing."

She twirled around once. "It's remarkable what a bubble bath and a new hairdo can do."

Danny quietly said, "You didn't cut your hair while you were back there, did you?"

She blinked. Dramatic and sexy in his dark tux, Danny stared at her. She wanted to stare right back. Some men were born to wear a tux, and he was one of them. Women would probably drool over him.

"No. It's an updo." She ventured a little farther into the living space. "I just swirled it around and pinned it up."

Charlotte said, "Well, you look very sophisticated."

Her eyes stole over to Danny again. She knew it would appear that she was hoping for his approval. But she wasn't. He had such presence and sex appeal with his black hair, dark eyes and tux that she couldn't stop staring at him. "That's the look I was going for."

Danny glanced at his watch. "We better get a move on or we'll arrive so late they'll think I decided not to come."

Something warm and fuzzy trembled through her. Forget what the press said. *She* was going out with the sexiest man alive.

Going out?

Not hardly. He was taking her to help her. She had to remember that.

Holding Rex, Charlotte walked with them to the elevator. "Have fun, you two." She picked up Rex's hand to wave it for him. "Say bye to Daddy and Marnie."

Marnie kissed his cheek. "Bye, sweetie."

Danny kissed his cheek. "Bye, big guy."

Charlotte's eyebrows rose. Marnie frowned. The weird feeling rippled through her again. They sounded like parents saying goodbye to their son. She took a breath, reminding herself to keep her wits about her.

The elevator door closed, and they headed down.

Staring straight ahead, Danny said, "You do look amazing."

Unwanted pleasure poured through her, and

she had to work not to groan. What was wrong with her? It would be so wrong for her to get a crush on her boss.

Oh, who was she kidding? She already did have a crush on him. She was simply wise enough not to act on it. Not only did she have an odd past—a secret—but Danny was rich, smart and funny. He could have his pick of women, and someone like her would not be at the top of his list. She wouldn't humiliate herself by taking anything he said as romantic.

"Thanks. I'm not one of those women who typically worries about appearances, but I didn't want to stand out."

"Oh, you'll still stand out."

The pleasure turned to a hiccup in her chest. It was impossible to miss the approval in his voice.

She chose to believe it was his way of saying she wouldn't embarrass him in front of his friends and glanced down at her dress. "In a black dress and pearls? Half the women there will be in a black dress."

The elevator door opened. "You'll still stand out." He peeked down at her. "You're stunning."

Happiness rose again, breath stealing and fierce. Their gazes locked. His dark eyes glowed.

The attraction she'd been fighting wasn't one-sided.

She swallowed hard. Even as her happiness turned to radiant joy, her stomach plummeted. She couldn't have him. If she ever fell in love, it would be with a normal guy, someone whose life wouldn't be affected by her kind of secret. But there was a more immediate issue. How the hell would she be able to work for this guy for *years* if they were attracted to each other?

She had to defuse this.

CHAPTER SIX

DANNY DIRECTED HER out of the elevator into the lobby, wrestling a case of desire so strong he reached up and loosened his collar.

He shouldn't have told her she was stunning. No. The stunning part was fine. It was the eye contact that had nearly done him in.

With her auburn hair pulled off her face, her eyes were a sharp, alluring green that almost made him stutter... If he'd been able to speak. But he'd held the contact so long, he could tell he'd unsettled her.

She frowned. "Was I that bad before? I know ponytails and yoga pants are comfortable, but I guess I looked like a slob."

He laughed and strode out of the building into the beautiful summer night, not only maintaining a discreet distance between them but mimicking her light tone. "No. You didn't look bad. You just look different tonight. You're going to be a big hit."

"I thought we were keeping this low-key?"

"That was the plan until you—" he motioned toward her dress "—got all fancied up."

She sniffed. "I'm telling you, there are going to be thirty women dressed exactly like this."

There weren't thirty. But there were enough women in black dresses that Danny had to admit defeat. Which made her laugh. Proving they'd succeeded in overcoming the awkward stare after he'd told her she looked stunning.

The gallery had been decorated with white lights and beach decor—wood that looked like it had washed up on a shore, pictures of the sun rising over the Atlantic, beach balls and seashells scattered around—but still it somehow looked posh and dripping with money.

She glanced around. "This is so beautiful."

He could relate. Six months ago, if someone had brought him here, he'd have reacted the same way. But right now, he couldn't seem to take his eyes off her. He told himself that was because she was clearly enjoying herself. So it was okay to notice the sparkle in her eyes.

"The woman who owns this gallery is known for her displays."

"Wow. It's amazing how the paintings match the displays."

* * *

She laughed again, but the farther they walked into the gallery, the more her chest tightened. Her father had always been drawn to the glamorous life. He could be here.

But a quick sweep of the area didn't find him. Or Roger. Or Roger's dad or mom.

Her shoulders loosened. Danny grabbed two flutes of champagne from the bar. "To your introduction to the world of investors."

She drew in a long breath. With the fear of running into someone from her past eliminated, she relaxed and took the glass he handed her and clinked it with his.

Everything was so elegant. Men in tuxes. Women in cocktail dresses. And for once she fit.

Of course, it didn't hurt that she was on the arm of the final Hinton heir.

No. Danny Manelli being a Hinton heir was irrelevant. He was without a doubt the best-looking guy in the room.

Out with her.

She felt all shivery and blamed it on the champagne, but she knew it was the night—with him.

He put his hand on the small of her back, directed her to another room of paintings, and she closed her eyes and savored. Wishes flurried through her brain like snowflakes on Christmas Eve. She wished she belonged here. That her dad hadn't deserted her but had brought her up in this world. She wished Danny would look at her again the way he had on the way to the limo. She wished she was free enough to turn and slide her arm beneath his, to walk nonchalantly from painting to painting, enjoying them. Enjoying *him.*

The last wish suddenly didn't seem so far out of line. No one from her past was in the gallery. She'd seen her dad once, on the street, on his typical Saturday morning jaunt to get a paper. She might not be free, but maybe she wasn't as ensnared as she believed.

Danny turned suddenly and they were face-to-face, so close that every cell in her body blossomed. Oh Lord. What would it be like to be allowed to flirt with him, to lure him to kiss her—

He pointed beyond her. "If we really want to make this a good trip for you, I need to introduce you to some people."

He stepped around her, easily heading toward a group closer to the door.

"Come on."

And just like that her moment was broken. She

drew a long breath. That was probably a good thing.

Wasn't it?

She worked for him. She had a complicated past. Plus, she had her eye on a good future.

But, oh, what would it be like to be Cinderella, to catch the Prince's eye and have one glorious evening—

Smoke and mirrors. That's what. She needed this job. Needed to start her own company to make enough money to change her life. She did not need a romance.

Danny introduced her to the McCallan clan, Jake and his wife, Avery, Seth and his wife, Harper, and Sabrina and her husband, Trent.

"Marnie is nanny for my son, Rex," Danny said casually. "She's thinking of starting her own nanny service in a few years."

Marnie picked up the cue. "It will be a little bit more of a boutique service. Maybe a service that doesn't actually nanny as much as provide a few afternoons a week of specialty services like art and music appreciation."

Beautiful blonde Sabrina McCallan Sigmund sighed. "So, our nanny could get an afternoon or two a week off?"

"Yes."

Sabrina's dark-haired, dark-eyed husband, Trent, said, "Interesting."

But Jake's gorgeous red-haired wife, Avery, laughed. "Our nanny would kiss your feet for coming up with something that would give her time off."

Marnie chuckled, and the conversation turned to the paintings around them and eventually all the McCallans drifted away.

Walking through the exhibit, admiring the paintings and displays, Danny introduced Marnie to a few other donors, older couples who didn't have kids and weren't quite as attuned to her idea as the McCallans. Still, Marnie's face shone. Her smile couldn't have been any wider. Starting a business clearly meant a lot to her.

The feeling returned. The click of rightness between them that reminded him of how well their lives meshed. She was smart and beautiful, everything he wanted in a woman. The perfection of it started a tingling in his chest. Every time he realized how well they fit, he took the leap from friends to more. And with it came the desire to hold her hand, to lean in close and laugh with her, to steal a kiss—

He fought to ignore it. "I told you there was no reason to be afraid."

She raised her eyes until their gazes connected. His chest tightened even more. Desire swam through his blood.

"These were just introductions. Everybody was being kind."

He wished he could kiss her. Wished he could tell her she was the most beautiful woman in the room.

He swallowed. "Speaking from experience, I can tell you that anyone with a child and a career isn't being kind about appreciating childcare."

"I suppose."

They'd looked at every picture. Had their fair share of champagne. Chitchatted with everyone he knew. And there was nothing else to see, no one else to meet…

But he didn't want the night to end. She looked glamorous and happy. It didn't seem right to whisk her home. He wanted to take her to dinner. To walk down Park Avenue on this warm night with the bright moon. To hold her hand and enjoy the city.

Wrong thoughts. Wrong wishes.

He shoved his hands in his pockets. "I guess it's time to go."

She set her champagne glass on the tray of a passing waiter. "Yeah. I'm feeling a little bit like Cinderella, and my coach is about to turn into a pumpkin."

The words to ask her to dinner sprang to his tongue. He bit them back and led her to the door. "Did you just call my limo a pumpkin?"

She laughed, but she glanced behind her longingly.

The urge to continue the night rippled through him.

Just twenty more minutes.

But he couldn't do that. He'd said they'd stay an hour. They'd stayed two. He hadn't mentioned dinner in his original invitation. He couldn't add it now—not when everything in him was warm from champagne and buzzed from the first fun outing he'd had since he'd discovered he'd been adopted. The emotions flowing through him were razor-sharp, as sexual as they were romantic, and probably wrong. The woman was his nanny. Not a date. His *nanny*. Someone he was helping.

The driver opened the limo door and they slid inside. The ride to his building didn't take long, and they exited quietly, walked through the lobby without a word and rode the elevator in silence.

Charlotte and Jace were waiting for them. Marnie hadn't met Charlotte's fiancé. Danny introduced Jace, who had thick dark hair and a build like a tank, then he offered him and Charlotte a drink, but both refused.

Charlotte snickered. "Jace has a big meeting in the morning with a rock star. They're the only ones able to get him out of bed on a Sunday. Even though he grouses about guarding them."

"They pay top dollar," Jace grumbled, but his ears turned red as he pressed the button for the elevator. It opened and then they were gone.

Danny and Marnie stood staring at the doors, alone in the suddenly silent space.

She pivoted to face him and said, "Good night. I had a great time. Thank you."

And everything inside Danny froze, except his brain, which spun out of control.

She *sounded like* a date, thanking him.

He *felt like* a guy who'd just had a great night with a woman he more than liked.

He *did* more than like her. Everything about her appealed to him. She loved his son, fit in his world and was so pretty his heart sat up and begged for him to kiss her.

Her eyes flickered and he suspected it was with

the same recognition he felt. Forget the fact that she was his nanny. Something more was happening between them.

The need to kiss her expanded into a fireball in his chest. He could imagine the feel of her soft lips, the smoothness of her cheek—

Seconds ticked off like hours. A debate raged in his brain—

Then the puppy raced up the hall, his nails clicking on the hardwood. Fat and eager for love, he slammed into Danny's ankles, bounced off and rolled ten feet back.

Marnie burst out laughing. "Oh, Wiggles," she said, walking over to pick him up. He licked her face a million times. "You have to get control of those paws."

She handed him to Danny. "I think he wants to go out."

Danny held her gaze, not quite able to shift gears from imagining the feel of her skin, the taste of her lips, to taking his dog out for a walk.

She smiled softly. "You might want to get a move on before he does something neither one of us will like."

That brought him back to reality. He had a child, a dog, more money than he needed and a weird father. Getting romantic with his nanny would only be trouble.

But, oh, he wanted to.

CHAPTER SEVEN

MARNIE WOKE THE next morning at five, the alarm on her phone sending soothing music to her until her eyes opened and she shut it off.

She always got up early, showered and dressed for the day before Rex woke at six. This morning, after that heart-stopping moment with Danny by the elevator, she'd stayed in bed a few seconds, the memory of it tiptoeing through her brain, not so much as pictures but as feelings, a shower of tingles as time spun out between them. Breathless anticipation. Fierce need, the likes of which she'd never felt.

Her common sense had told her to look away… walk away. But the fanciful part of herself that she'd believed to be long dead pleaded with her to stay. To wait. To see if he would kiss her.

She thought of her secret and shook her head. What difference did her secret make? If he'd kissed her, it would have been once and only because the night had been so romantic. It wasn't like they'd start something.

And even if they did? No one had been overly interested in him the night before. The press in attendance had flocked around the McCallans, sponsors of the event. The artist, Sally McMillen, never came to her showings. So the sponsors got the spotlight.

She and Danny Manelli had just been two attendees.

She hadn't seen her dad. Or Roger. Or his parents.

Another piece of her fear drifted away. And maybe it was time? Her bad past was a decade behind her. Something inside her yearned for a normal life. A life where she could be herself. Be loved—

Finally loved.

Which was exactly what had gotten her into trouble the first time. The life she'd had with her mom in the apartment in Brooklyn had been spare and sometimes lonely. She'd just wanted to belong again—

And that had ended disastrously.

She rolled out of bed, showered, dressed and walked into the kitchen to get things ready for Rex, but suddenly the sound of his crying made its way from his room, up the hall, to the kitchen area.

She dropped his sippy cup to the center island and raced to his room. Turning on the light, she said, "Hey, buddy. What's wrong? How come you're up early?"

He all but leaped into her arms when she reached for him. She squeezed him tight before laying him on the changing table. Still, he sobbed. She took care of his diaper, leaving his pajamas on. In case he spilled some breakfast, these were already dirty, and his daytime clothes would be safe.

She pulled him from the table into her arms again. "It's okay."

"Why is he crying?"

She turned at the sound of Danny's voice and her heart tumbled. Whiskers covered his chin and cheeks. His hair was sexily mussed. Pajama pants hung on his lean hips. He wasn't wearing a shirt, showing off a perfect chest. The kind of chest a woman could lay her head on while she listened to the slow beat of his heart.

"I'm not sure." Her words came out breathless, and she hoped Danny thought she was whispering. "Go back to bed. I'll take him to the kitchen for breakfast. Maybe he's just hungry."

"I'll help." He reached for Rex. As he leaned in to take him, their gazes met and all the air whooshed out of her lungs. Her mind went back to those few minutes in front of the elevator the night before. A sense of unfinished business skimmed her nerve endings.

His dark eyes flashed. Rex flung himself into his father's arms.

He caught him just in time. "Hey, buddy. What's the matter?"

He only cried louder and harder, but he snuggled against his father's shoulder.

Danny headed for the kitchen. "How about some milk?"

Marnie raced to the kitchen before them, grabbed the sippy cup and filled it, then handed it to Danny. He gave it to Rex, who tossed it on the floor. When the cap popped off, milk flew everywhere.

"I think this kid likes seeing milk on the floor."

Marnie laughed with relief at the joke. "If he won't take milk, there's something wrong. I'm guessing he's getting a tooth. Let me feel along his gums."

As soon as she ran her finger along his gums, Rex settled. She felt the bumps of a molar. "Yep. It's a tooth."

Rex sniffed.

Danny snuggled his son. "What do we do?"

"First, let's see if eating something will help him. Sometimes chewing numbs the gums. If not, we can use some over-the-counter pain reliever."

Danny squeezed his eyes shut. "His mother told me about this. I forgot."

"Did she by any chance send over some pain reliever?"

"Yes."

"Then we're good. We'll feed him, maybe take him to the park for a walk to distract him, and just play with him hard-core to keep his mind off things."

Danny sighed. "Okay. Seems like a plan."

She took the toddler from his arms. "You go change out of your wet clothes and get the pain reliever. I'll see if I can get him to eat a banana or some oatmeal. We don't want to give him meds on an empty stomach."

"Okay. Good. I'll be right back."

Rex ate the banana and some oatmeal, while Marnie cleaned up the milk mess. They gave him a dose of the pain reliever and Marnie changed him into a T-shirt and board shorts with little tennis shoes for their trip to take Wiggles outside.

They walked through the park with Rex happily settled in his stroller. After an hour, with neither Rex nor Wiggles looking eager to return to the penthouse, they found a park bench. Watching everything around him, Rex chewed on a soft plastic toy.

"Is that good for him?"

"Yes. It works the gums and as I mentioned before, sometimes chewing numbs them. Don't worry. I made sure it was clean."

He caught her gaze. "I wasn't worried. You know what you're doing."

"Thanks."

She looked away from his mesmerizing eyes. He wanted to say something. It was all right there in his dark orbs. Even as part of her waited breathlessly, she hoped that he wouldn't. Everything was happening so fast. And he was her *boss*. She had plans for her life. Not to mention that a longing like this had derailed her once before, resulting in a secret that always rode in the back of her brain.

"I had a good time last night."

She glanced to the right, away from him, long enough to squeeze her eyes shut for a few seconds before she looked back at him. "I did too."

"I almost kissed you at the elevator."

"I know."

"I want you to know I won't." He pulled in a

breath. "I need you too much. And I don't want to be a cliché."

She laughed. "Cliché?"

"You know…guy who falls for the young good-looking nanny."

She couldn't remember the last time someone had called her good-looking. Her mom had told her she looked nice before she went out. Even Danny had called her stunning the night before. But this was different. His praise was all encompassing, not a passing compliment.

"What about me? Nanny who falls for her good-looking boss. We'd both be clichés."

"Maybe the problem is that we're both good-looking?"

She laughed and playfully tapped his upper arm. "Stop."

"No. I'm serious. I almost hired an older woman. Not that she wasn't attractive. But she didn't make me want to kiss her."

She gaped at him. "I am not having this conversation!"

"Hey, this isn't just about you and Mary Poppins."

"Mary Poppins?"

"She sort of reminded me of Mary Poppins.

But this isn't just about you and her. You said I was good-looking."

"You're ridiculous."

"No. What I am is happy. Ever since you came to help me with Rex, I've felt it. And I worry that what I think is attraction might actually be relief."

Her brain stalled. "What?"

"Relief. You know… I'm so glad to have one part of my life settling that I might be attaching the wrong meaning to it. I have a crazy dad, parents who didn't tell me I was adopted, and a woman who didn't tell me she was pregnant. My trust issues have trust issues. I don't have time or space for a relationship. Yet this feeling comes naturally. So, I figure it has to be relief."

She peered over at him. "Oh." She thought for a second. "I'm also making really good money with you. Better than I ever had. You're helping me reach phase two of my career. There's a bit of relief on my part too."

"Add that we're good-looking to all these feelings of relief and we might be imagining something that's not there."

Disappointment tried to spike. She wouldn't let it. It was ridiculous to long for something that wasn't right. "Yeah."

"See? I think I hit the nail on the head. And

you didn't want to talk about this," he scoffed. "If we hadn't, we'd have hung around worrying about something we don't need to worry about."

Like a past that might surface. A dad who didn't want her. A mom who was always a drink away from destroying her life.

Looking at it objectively like that, she realized she'd spent her life mired in fear. "I do have a history of that."

"Well, now that you're working for me, we're going to stop it."

She grinned. "I feel like that might be happening. You know… I love Rex. I'm comfortable in your house. No one seems to think I'm out of place on your street, at the bakery, walking Wiggles. It's all—" she laughed "—a relief."

"So, we agree? We're good for each other in so many ways that it feels romantic but it's not."

"That has to be it. We're both too smart to do something stupid."

"We can go back and eat lunch like normal people."

"We did skip breakfast."

"Another reason to stop at the bakery. And this time get two Danish."

She laughed. "What?"

"We're friends now. There's no reason for pretense. If you want two Danish, get two Danish. If you want a bagel, get a bagel. Let's be ourselves."

The idea of being herself sent another wave of relief rippling through her.

She'd been in hiding for ten years. Not letting herself be or do much of anything. Now, suddenly she was a twenty-six-year-old woman. The past seemed far away. Especially with no one having had reason to dredge it up for a decade. Her dad didn't matter. Her mom had been sober for fourteen years, thanks to Alcoholics Anonymous.

Had she really worried for nothing all these years?

She rose from the bench. The colors of the sky seemed brighter. Rex laughed at Wiggles, who whipped over to lick his cheek.

"Since we're being ourselves, I'll admit I'm starving. Let's go now."

Danny rose too. "Bakery it is."

The weekend passed quickly. Talking about their feelings seemed to work for Marnie. She was light, happy. Rex made it to Monday despite his sore gums. But at breakfast, Danny felt odd. All day Sunday, he'd reminded himself that his happiness around Marnie was relief. But at a certain point he had to admit that wasn't true. He liked her and he'd basically warned her off.

He should have kissed her Saturday night.

If she'd quit, he could have asked her for a date.

If she hadn't quit, they'd have figured something out.

But he'd taken the high road. And now look where he was. Watching the woman who filled his heart with joy play mother to his child. He might have only known her a few weeks, but they fit.

And he'd blown it.

It didn't help that he spent Monday in court and returned home exhausted and grumpy. Rex spilled his juice. Wiggles peed on the floor. Marnie handled it all like the pro she was.

She retired to her room after putting Rex to bed. Danny walked to the family room, a large room in the back with a big screen TV and enough toys and games to entertain fifty people.

He tuned the television to a baseball game, racked the balls on the pool table and grabbed a cue stick from the holder.

He shot two games, groaning at the ineptitude of his favorite baseball team and trying to unwind.

"Hey."

His gaze shot up when Marnie entered the room. "I'm sorry if I was too loud. I forgot I'm on your side of the penthouse."

She meandered a bit closer. "It's okay. I couldn't hear you, but…" She bit her lower lip, a habit he'd observed she indulged when she was nervous. "Well, at dinner I noticed you were stressed."

He straightened, searched for his next shot, then leaned over to take it. "That's a natural result of spending a day in court. You have two sides who both believe they're right." He slid the stick between his fingers and smacked the cue ball into three other balls with a resounding crack. "I handle mostly estates so the only times I enter a courtroom are when relatives are fighting over money."

He hit the cue ball again. The red ball flew into a pocket. He drew a satisfied breath. "Fighting families are the worst."

"I'll bet." She plopped down on the sofa, tucking one leg under her butt and laying one arm along the back pillows. It was sweet that she wanted to talk him out of his stress, but she had no idea that the more he saw her, the more he wanted her, and right now she was playing with fire.

"But, honestly, I don't have much family. My

mom was an orphan. My dad single-minded. We didn't host relatives for Thanksgiving. Our guests were his clients."

He longed to talk about his day, hear about her life. But wasn't that part of the problem? The connection they were making lured him in to want more.

He took another shot. "That sounds lovely."

"It wasn't." She paused a beat. "What about you?"

He looked up. Her eyes were warm, her gaze friendly. If he didn't answer, she'd know something was wrong.

"Before I met Leni and Charlotte, I didn't have any brothers and sisters. My parents were never chosen by another birth mother. I did have oodles of cousins though."

She came to attention. "Really? What's that like?"

A memory of a week at the lake popped into his head, and—amazingly—he laughed. "Chaotic. There was only one girl cousin and we terrorized her."

"You didn't!"

"Hey, we were boys in the woods. If we found a snake, it wasn't our fault that we wanted to show it off."

She laughed.

Finished with his game, he should have gone to his room. Instead, with his muscles loosening and the stress of the day slipping away, he motioned to the table. Just like always, being with her did something to him. Something he liked. Something he needed.

"Do you play?"

She looked at her fingernails. "A bit."

"Don't tell me you're a ringer."

She pushed off the sofa. "No. But I have my days."

She chose a stick and he let her break. She ended up with the striped balls and had four put away before he got his first turn.

Focused, he worked to get three in the pockets. Then she bent across the table to shoot and her yoga pants outlined her butt.

He took a quick breath and blew it out slowly.

She only sank one ball before she lost her turn. As he studied the table, she said, "What else happens in court?"

She had a good idea keeping the conversation neutral, but it didn't work when she used that breathless voice.

"Lawyers try to trip up witnesses from the opposing side." He took a shot, missed and wasn't the slightest surprised.

She leaned across the table again. He looked at the ceiling. "Your job is essentially tripping people up?"

"No. My job is looking for loopholes, mistakes in thinking, and law, precedents, that support my position."

"You're a trickster."

"No!" He thought of his dad and fought the urge to ball his hands into fists. "I'm the one who uncovers tricksters."

"Much more interesting."

The breathless voice was back. Most of the balls were in the pocket. Both would shoot for the eight. He suddenly wished he could stand back and just watch her. Her movements were easy, fluid. Her proficiency at the game a total turn-on.

She tried for the eight, missed. He ambled to her side of the table as she walked to his. They met at a corner that she'd taken too sharply and suddenly they were in front of each other, almost brushing, both breathing funny.

They'd had the talk about how they weren't going to pursue anything romantic, but after a day in court with his nerves strung tight, his defenses worn down… He couldn't for the life of him remember why he'd agreed to that—

No. He couldn't remember why he'd *suggested* that.

Familiar feelings rumbled through him. Primal. Quiet. Resurrecting an instinct so deep it merged body and soul.

He was suddenly the man he'd been before he'd met his dad and discovered he had a child. For thirty seconds, he was just a guy with needs. A hunger for the pretty girl in front of him.

"I thought we weren't going to do this."

His voice came out rough as he said, "I can't for the life of me remember why."

"Neither one of us wants to be a cliché."

"If that's our only reason, it's not a good one."

CHAPTER EIGHT

MARNIE'S HEART POUNDED, making her chest tight enough she worried it would burst. They were so close she swore she could hear his heart beating. Everything had been good over the weekend, then he'd come home tired and out of sorts and something inside her had yearned to make him feel better.

She whispered, "You're sure it's not a good one?"

His head began to lower. "Very."

When their lips met, a symphony of longing sang through her blood. Almost powerful enough to drown out her fears, it filled her heart, wove through her soul. Their connection was strong, but their attraction was stronger. She didn't know how to fight it. Even when she reminded herself that he lived in a different world, part of her scoffed that he was a simple billionaire. Not one of the guys who attracted attention. And any private time she got with him would be worth it.

He deepened the kiss, his tongue delving into

the recesses of her mouth. The longing intensified, whooshing through her, stealing her breath. Thoughts of where this was going, what they were doing should have terrified her. Instead, they stoked the flames of the fire.

He pulled away unexpectedly. She blinked up at him. Something wild and wonderful shivered between them. For a breath, she considered springing to her tiptoes and getting them back to kissing...but something serious had settled in his eyes.

"I think we both know where this was going and we both need to think about it some more."

Drowsy, confused, she stepped back. After a second for his words to sink in, to remind her of consequences and ramifications, she said, "Yeah."

He ran his hand through his hair. "I'm going to my room now."

"Me too."

As if he couldn't take his eyes off her, he started backing toward the door. "See you in the morning."

She nodded.

He left, and she stared at the door, her arousal subsiding, her needs mixing and mingling then breaking apart when she added her past and

everything didn't exactly mesh. Not only was
he sexy and amazing, but he was a good person.
Genuinely good. And she should be thankful he'd
been levelheaded.

Even thoughts of his control sent warmth cas-
cading through her. He could have taken advantage of her. She'd had that happen too many times
to count, when the hole in her life left by her
missing father had caused her to go looking for
love all the wrong ways. His respect for her filled
her eyes with tears and her soul with yearning.

For something she couldn't have. Because she'd
made a mistake. And that mistake followed her.

The next morning, she continued her routine of
showering and getting things ready for Rex before he woke at six. She changed him, put him in
his highchair and was fixing his breakfast when
Danny walked into the kitchen for his coffee.

Her breath filled with something so light and
bemusing it fluttered in her chest. Trying not to
look like a smitten fool, she monitored her smile,
kept it a reasonable lift of her lips, not a beaming
grin. "Good morning."

He bypassed the coffeepot, walked over and
put his forearm around her waist, pulling her to
him. His lips met hers quickly, hotly, and her
limbs turned to jelly.

He broke the kiss but didn't release her. Staring into her eyes, he said, "Good morning."

Her mind went blank. No matter how wrong, something inside her desperately wanted this.

"Everything happened so fast last night and escalated before either one of us was ready. So, I thought we'd introduce…you know…'it' into our routine. So it isn't shocking and overpowering."

Which made perfect sense. Maybe if she had a chance to get accustomed to the idea of something between them, it wouldn't seem at odds with her life. At odds with her past. A past that had been buried for ten long years.

After a few seconds she said, "That's a heck of a way to start the day."

He laughed and walked to the coffeemaker. "And that's what I like about you. Right there. You are so wonderfully honest."

His words like a punch in the gut, her good feelings shattered like glass. She wasn't honest. She hadn't told him her secret—

"Or maybe it's not that you're honest. It's more like you're yourself."

That she had been. She was absolutely herself. He'd let her be herself. In fact, he'd encouraged it.

"Court again today," he said, leaning against the counter, looking sexy and sophisticated in his white shirt and black trousers, as his cup of coffee brewed. "I'm leaving early to get some time in the office to prepare."

"For the fighting family?"

"Yes. I got to thinking last night that if I was as good of a lawyer as I think I am, I should be able to find a way to settle this. Today. Before another long, frustrating day in front of a judge."

He hadn't been thinking about their kiss?

She'd spent hours tossing and turning.

But maybe that was better? Prioritizing was a good thing. And too much passion too soon might ruin everything. Which was what he'd been trying to say after he'd kissed her.

Oh heavens.

He was right again. He was always right. Doing the correct thing. While she was crazy, floundering, picking apart every move, everything he'd said. And why? Because she didn't want to get burned again?

Even if what they started didn't pan out, he wouldn't burn her. He wouldn't embarrass her. He wouldn't take pictures of her while she was sleeping—

A chill raced down her spine. None of that had entered her mind with Roger. That's why she overanalyzed now. She carefully considered every man she dated before even the idea of sleeping with them came into the situation.

But with Danny all her rules were going out the window. Trust had been swift, easy.

Did she have any idea what she was doing with him?

What she might be doing to herself?

He left without taking Wiggles for a walk, which was fine. Maybe even good. Fresh air and sunshine might clear her head.

Dressing Rex in denim shorts, a T-shirt and his fancy tennis shoes, she told Wiggles not to panic. They would be going out soon.

With Rex ready and in the small umbrella stroller, easier for her when she was alone with the puppy and the baby, she fastened Wiggles's leash, then they piled into the elevator.

In the lobby, the doorman said, "Good morning."

She returned his greeting and soon they were out on the sidewalk.

The second she stepped into the sun, she felt better. With Wiggles's leash attached to the arm of the stroller, she put on her big sunglasses— a gift she'd bought herself while shopping for her art gala dress—and headed toward the nearest park.

Rex grinned happily. Wiggles trotted along. And all things returned to normal. Her nerves stabilized. What she felt for Danny wasn't pressing or confusing. It sat above her brain like a happy little rainbow.

She found a bench in the park, turned Rex's stroller to face her so they could chitchat and loosened Wiggles's leash to let him roam a bit.

"This is nice."

Rex said, "Nice."

"Oh, I see you're catching on to some new words."

"Words."

She laughed. "You're adorable."

He grinned.

She took a breath and leaned back. The warm sun beat down on her, soothing her soul. The night before, Danny had said they both needed time to think this through. Not while in crazy panic mode, but the way Danny seemed to analyze things. Slowly. Deliberately.

She went back to the beginning. From the way she'd thought he was gorgeous when she'd met him to the way she'd gone to the game room the night before. Nervous, tense, he'd needed to relax. She knew she could help him.

She *wanted* to help him.

There were genuine feelings there. Not just attraction, but emotion. She couldn't deny it.

Danny was obviously wealthier than her typical employers, who were usually two-income executive parents, working to get rich, not already rich. Yet, he was a normal guy. Probably because he'd been raised middle-class.

Score one for him.

But score one for her too. She'd adjusted to his lifestyle rather easily. She'd slid into his world as if she was made to be there.

And maybe she was?

They were a normal girl and guy finding love on Park Avenue.

Her fears melting like butter in the morning sun and the wonder of actually being able to have these kinds of emotions, she giggled. Rex grinned at her.

And that was another thing. She and Rex had become fast friends. He snuggled her and took to her as if he'd liked her immediately.

Second score for her. If she and Danny started something, there'd be no worry about Rex liking her.

Of course, if their romance failed, Rex would lose her.

Drat. That took away one of their points.

Wiggles pulled on the leash, yanking the stroller and Marnie bounced up. If the direction of the leash was correct, the crazy dog had gotten himself caught in a bush. She grabbed the stroller handles and headed toward the bush. Pushing the stroller around it, she said, "Hey, you crazy dog—"

She stopped dead. On the bench across the walking path was her dad. He looked older than he had the day she'd gotten the glimpse of him as he walked by her and Danny. Older and thin. As if he'd been ill. He also wore a sweater on a hot end-of-July morning.

Wiggles barked and he glanced up, over the rim of reading glasses. He set his newspaper on the bench beside him and speared her with a look. "Oh, for heaven's sake."

Marnie's lungs froze. Her tongue numbed. She could only stare as he glared at her.

From out of nowhere, a young guy in a T-shirt and jeans reached into the bush, untangled the leash, then pulled Wiggles out and handed him to her.

"Here you go, ma'am."

She might have stumbled over the word *ma'am*, but her frozen tongue wouldn't work. The guy walked away, and she stared at her father.

With a heavy sigh, he folded his newspaper and rose from the bench. "If you can't manage both a kid and a dog, you shouldn't come to the park."

Memories from when she'd lived with him cascaded in her brain. Being yelled at. Being criticized. Both reasons her mom drank. Every time her parents went out, somehow her mom had screwed things up. Said the wrong thing to someone important. Danced too much or not enough. Her dad would return home disappointed. Her mother had walked to the bar. Her mom might have been an alcoholic, but her dad had driven her over the edge. Even at twelve Marnie had known that.

Staring at his grouchy face, it seemed he hadn't changed. If he had even an ounce of compassion, she'd never seen it.

Newspaper under his arm, he stormed off.

She licked her suddenly dry lips. The second time in fourteen years that he'd seen her, and he'd scolded her.

Why was she surprised?

Why did she care!

CHAPTER NINE

DANNY CAME HOME to an energetic puppy, a happy little boy and an extremely quiet nanny.

Damn. The kiss that morning might have been over-the-top. But he hadn't been able to help himself. He was the kind of guy who went after what he wanted, and he wanted her.

He'd thought his plan to casually introduce romance was a good one. Clearly, though, he'd pushed a bit too hard. He would draw back. Give her space. After all, he wasn't in any position to rush things. The slower they took this, the more chance she'd learn to trust him.

"Hi." He headed back to his bedroom. "Give me two minutes to change and I'll call to have dinner delivered."

"I actually made something for dinner."

He stopped halfway to the master. "You did?"

She shrugged. "Just veal cutlets."

He ventured a few steps back. "*Just* veal cutlets."

"Yeah."

"Okay."

Her usually bright green eyes were dull. Her voice one shade above somber.

Something was really bothering her, and the only new thing in their world was him kissing her. Still, he wasn't sorry. If she was, all she had to do was say so. She hadn't ever been shy about telling him anything.

But dinner was quiet. She picked at her food.

And damn it, he wanted her to like him.

He thought about it as he loaded the dishwasher. Maybe ten hours away from him had her thinking too much? Yes, he'd told her they needed to think this through, but he felt like defense counsel when they didn't get an opportunity for rebuttal.

They needed to talk. He might not have been able to get her to open up yet, but he could, if they spent a little time together.

"Hey, how about a movie tonight?"

"A movie?"

"I'm subscribed to enough services that we're sure to find something you'll like."

Her face perked up. "That would be nice."

Okay. Good. She wasn't averse to spending time with him. But something was wrong.

"And I swear. No kissing this time."

She laughed, then met his gaze. "I liked the kiss."

"I *loved* the kiss. But if you want to go with *like*, that's fine. I'll wear you down."

She laughed again.

That was more like it.

They watched the movie as two friends, no kiss this time, and the next morning, she was herself again. The only thing that had changed between them was that they'd spent two hours together watching a movie and he *hadn't* kissed her.

He all but decided to totally back off, but by Friday morning her good humor had completely returned.

Saturday morning, she suggested a couple of hours in the park and another stop at the bakery.

"Sounds great!"

Thrilled that she was happy again, he helped her pack up Wiggles and Rex. But when she turned right out of their building rather than left, he put a hand on her arm.

"Park's that way."

She nodded. "I know. There's another park just up the street, though."

"It's not *just* up the street. It's blocks up the street. By the time we stroll Rex that far, Wiggles's bladder will have exploded." He shifted his voice from shocked to cajoling. "Come on. I worked all week. I need bench time in the sun."

He turned the stroller to go in their usual direction and though she sort of smiled in agreement, he noticed her stiffen. When they got to the bench, she sat cautiously.

After setting the brake on Rex's stroller, he lowered himself beside her with a satisfied, "Ah… What a week."

She tucked a strand of her long hair behind her ear. "Yeah."

He might have spent three days in court, but he'd also kissed her. They'd played pool, watched a movie. Yet her, "Yeah," was cautious.

"I mean, I love being a lawyer, helping other people unravel problems, but fighting families get to me."

She shifted on the bench. He knew her parents were divorced and almost cursed himself for the dumb remark.

"Though, I'm beginning to think all families are crazy."

She sniffed. He felt a little better and decided maybe he shouldn't talk. Up until kissing her, their relationship had developed naturally. Then he'd kissed her and become an idiot.

So, no. No more forced discussions. From here on out conversations would develop naturally.

An older gentleman in a sweater walked by. He didn't say anything, but Danny could swear he heard the man growl.

Marnie froze for a few seconds before she caught Wiggles's leash and rose. "You know what? I'm tired. Could we go back?" Her gaze moved toward the guy, then jerked back again.

Danny glanced from her to the old man, who had taken a seat on the bench behind the bush, and this time he froze. He recognized him. At least, he thought he did.

He whispered, "Is that your dad?"

She wouldn't look at him. "He saw Wiggles get caught in the bush the other day." She paused, sucked in a breath. "He didn't know who I was."

"Is that why he growled as he walked by?"

She shrugged. "He told me if I couldn't handle both a kid and a dog, I shouldn't come to the park."

Danny's eyes widened in disbelief at the man's rudeness. "He *said* that?"

"Let's just go."

"No. Even if he wasn't your dad, this is a public park." Without a thought, he charged across the path. "Did you yell at my nanny the last time she was here?"

He didn't look up from his newspaper.

"Hey, I'm talking to you." He shoved the paper down a bit so he could see the old man's face. "This is a public park and my nanny is one of the best. She put herself through university and plans to start her own agency. She didn't deserve your criticism. I'm not exactly sure why you thought you had the right to yell at her, but you didn't."

He turned and stormed back to the stroller, the dog and wide-eyed Marnie. He caught her arm with one hand and the stroller with the other, glad Wiggles's leash was tied to the handle and pushed them out of the park.

When they reached the sidewalk, he let go of her, and they headed up the street as if nothing had happened.

"I'm sorry if I overstepped."

She didn't say anything, just looked at him, absolute shock written all over her face.

"I don't usually have a temper."

"That was hardly a temper. It was…a rebuttal."

He laughed, and they walked the rest of the way to his building in complete silence. He might have laughed, but after a few seconds, he realized her voice had been somber, nowhere near happy. He expected her resignation when they stepped off the elevator. Instead, she took Rex back to the nursery. When she came out, she walked to him, slid her hand around his neck, brought his face to hers and kissed him.

Her mouth met his chastely but she'd surprised him so much that instinct took over, and he opened his lips, letting the two of them fall naturally into the emotion that both pleased and bedeviled him. Sensations washed over him. Need. Hunger.

And a link that reached into his soul and filled it with something indescribable. He didn't have an idea in hell what was happening to him. He just knew he liked it.

She pulled away from the long, slow, erotic kiss. "Do you know how long I've wanted to say something like that to him?"

"Why haven't you?"

"In my head, I'm still twelve."

"Well, now he knows you're not twelve anymore. That you've gotten a degree and intend to start a company."

She laughed, ran her hand through her hair. "That was surreal."

It was for him too. Not standing up for her to her dad. But feeling things so intensely they caused him to act before he thought. "Want to go back and yell at him again?"

Her laugh deepened, filled with relief and joy. "No. I'm good." She took a quick breath. "I'm really good." She looked around as if seeing his condo for the first time.

"You're sure you're okay?"

"I think I need to go see my mom."

His breath puffed out on a sigh, but he caught it. She didn't want to talk to him about what had happened that morning. She wanted to talk to her mom. "What?"

"I haven't taken any time off in a while. At least no time out of the house." She shrugged. "I think she needs to know I've seen my dad."

He ran his hand along the back of his neck. "Yeah. Okay. I get that."

She nodded and ran back to her room. In seconds, she reappeared. Still in the yoga pants and T-shirt, what he considered her nanny attire, but holding her purse with one hand as she slid her big sunglasses on with the other.

"See you."

He said, "Yeah. See you," and watched her leave. But the strangest feeling passed through him. All the wicked suspicions that had overwhelmed him the first time she'd seen her dad in the park and told him—even though they didn't know each other.

Part of him understood that Marnie would want to talk to her mom about seeing her dad. But once again, it suddenly all seemed incredibly coincidental.

Could she have really "accidentally" gotten a job close to where her dad lived?

And was it really an accident that she kept running into him?

He shook his head. *Was he crazy?* He and Marnie were like two peas in a pod—

They meshed. Like she was made for him—

Why did that suddenly strike him as odd, too?

Why did it sound an alarm bell?

The memory of Marnie telling him she'd seen her dad the first time came back like a scene from a movie.

She'd been so open about it. Up-front. But had she needed to tell him? At that point they'd only known each other a day—

Then she'd seen her dad again that week and today on their walk. Rather coincidental.

Sure, weeks had gone by. And, yes, her wealthy father could live on Park Avenue. But what if she'd known? What if she'd wanted to edge her way into her dad's life? What better way than to work near where he lived?

And what better thing than to have a smitten employer approach him, tell him things, pave the way, so she didn't have to?

Then she thanks him with a kiss and races off to report to her mom? Maybe to make plans of some sort to extort money—

He dropped his head to his hands.

Damn.

Had he just been conned?

Or had being Mark Hinton's son officially made him crazy?

As crazy as his father, who always said money ruined trust?

Always.

CHAPTER TEN

"OF COURSE, YOU'RE SUSPICIOUS." Danny's sister Leni sat on the paisley chair across from the sofa where Danny sat. "You're a newly rich guy who didn't merely discover he was adopted. Your biological dad also may or may not have faked his death after poking into your life enough to discover you had a son, who you are now raising alone. In a few months, you went from a middle-class single guy to a wealthy dad. And a very eligible bachelor."

Danny sat back. Leni had called him right after Marnie left, said she had cookies for Rex and was in the lobby.

Befuddled, he'd let her up. Still, he'd forced himself to behave normally through making coffee, happily taking one of the cookies she'd brought for him and Rex and even making initial chitchat.

But when she'd asked about Marnie, he couldn't quite fake it. He'd shaken his head, as his fears had spilled out of his mouth. "I'd been suspicious that first walk in the park when she casually told me—a virtual stranger—that she'd seen her dad—the dad who abandoned her and her mom. So why the hell hadn't I listened to myself?" He squeezed his eyes shut, then popped them open again. "I think I've snapped."

"Or..." Petite Leni with her long brown hair and big eyes filled with wisdom, leaned forward on the paisley chair. "You could give yourself the benefit of the doubt. A lot of things that happened with Marnie do seem coincidental."

"I thought we were soul mates or something because we'd been able to talk so easily, when the whole time she might have been setting me up."

"So what if she'd found her dad before she'd gotten the job with you? So what if she's taking this opportunity to meet him or get to know him? Does that really impact how she cares for Rex?"

He combed his hand through his hair. "Not so far. She's a great nanny. Rex loves her."

"And you have no proof that she tricked you?"

"Just suspicions."

"Charlotte and I both went through something like this. When you first find out you're not who you think you are, you question everything that's happened in your life. Plus, Mark made you attorney for his estate, as if you'd earned it, then you discovered he's your biological dad and *he* was setting you up." She shook her head and laughed. "I'd worry about you if you weren't overly suspicious."

He snorted. "Yeah. That's a valid point."

"You're probably right on track with where Charlotte and I were when we discovered we were Hinton heirs." The sound of Rex crying came through the monitor. "Let's go get the baby. We'll eat cookies and play. Forget all this."

"We'll spoil his dinner."

"Okay, we'll give him one cookie and play." She rose from the chair. "What time is your nanny coming back?"

"She didn't say."

And maybe that was his real worry. That she *wasn't* coming back—that their wonderful, explosive kiss had been a goodbye kiss. She'd seen her dad. The old man knew she'd gotten her degree and had plans for her future. Now she could move on.

Maybe even make a call or two to the people he'd introduced her to at Sally McMillen's showing.

He sucked in a breath. He couldn't figure out if he was the world's biggest chump or the most suspicious guy on the planet.

But he did know getting involved with a woman he barely knew, someone he *employed* had been reckless.

"You're a Hinton heir," Leni continued as they walked the hall to Rex's room. "As attorney for the estate, you warned me and Charlotte to watch ourselves. That people would befriend us because of the money. Friends would behave oddly. There's a weird satisfaction in getting to return your warning. Watch yourself."

He nodded, but sadness gripped him. It took a second or two of thinking, but he realized why Leni's warning made him sad. Marnie was the nicest, sweetest woman he'd ever met. He was the one with the problem. A crazy biological father. A bunch of doubts and suspicions. The weirdness of finding out he wasn't who he thought he was—

How could he blame Marnie, be suspicious of her, when he was the one with all the issues?

Marnie raced up the stairs to her mom's apartment and used her key to let herself in. "Mom?"

"In here." Her mother appeared at her bedroom door. Tall and willowy with auburn hair sprinkled with gray and wearing jeans and a loose purple top, Judy Olsen said, "What's up?"

"Come into the living room." Furnished with

a yellow floral sofa and chair her mom had pur-
chased secondhand, the combination living room/
family room was as far away from Danny Manelli's sleek, sophisticated main room as it could
get. Windows were covered with yellow drapes
and blinds—also out-of-date. But everything was
clean and light, pretty and airy, like her mom.

Judy took a seat on the sofa, beside her knitting.
Marnie fell into the chair. "I saw Dad."

Her mom blinked. "Oh?"

"He must live near my employer's penthouse,
because I've seen him a few times at the park
where I take Rex and Wiggles."

One eyebrow rose. "Wiggles?"

"Not the important part of the story, Mom."

"I know, but frankly I'd rather not hear about
your dad." She closed her eyes, took a breath and
popped them open again. "But I promised myself that if you wanted to have a relationship with
him, I wouldn't stop you."

Marnie shook her head. "He seems exactly as
he was when he left. Miserable."

"I always blamed myself for that. You know…
having a drunk for a wife embarrassed and hu-
miliated him, so he was grouchy."

"Well, I think you can forgive yourself and
move on. Living on Park Avenue with you being

in no way involved in his life, he's still a… I won't say the word in polite conversation."

Her mom laughed.

"The first time I saw him, he didn't notice me. The second time, Wiggles was caught in a bush, and he scolded me, saying if I couldn't handle a kid and a dog I shouldn't go to the park."

"He didn't help you?"

"No. Some guy strolling by pulled Wiggles out. All Dad did was criticize."

"Hmmm. Sounds like him."

"Then this morning, my employer was with me and I had to tell him the story and he stormed over and told Dad never to harass his nanny again…or something."

Judy laughed.

"But that's not the best part. Danny told Dad I was smart and had graduated university and was planning on starting my own company and didn't deserve his comments."

"Wow."

"It was like… I don't know? Getting the chance to show him who I was, that his leaving hadn't ruined me. All without the nasty business of fallout. He doesn't care about some nanny in the park…but I got my say."

"It probably did feel good."

"It felt like closure, and I have Danny Manelli to thank."

Her mom's eyes narrowed, and she studied Marnie's face. "You told your new boss a heck of a lot about yourself."

She shrugged. "He's easy to talk to." And kiss. And in general, be around. But her mom didn't need to know that.

"What else did you tell him?"

Marnie sat back. "You mean, did I tell him about Roger Martin?"

She didn't even try to hide it. "Yes."

"No. Because it wasn't relevant. I told Danny about Dad because I hadn't wanted to go to that side of the park…the side where I'd seen Dad before. I ended up having to explain."

"I'm still not sure how telling your dad about your successes crept into defending you."

Marnie quietly said, "It made sense at the time."

"Oh, sweetie, don't be angry. I'm just concerned. In a few weeks, you've all but told your boss your entire life story."

"We live together, eat together, care for his son together—"

"And you're getting close?"

She took a breath, praying for patience. "It's hard not to."

Judy ran her hands down her face. "Your dad showed you that there are some men who will take what they want and when things don't go their way, they bolt. They don't talk. They don't try to fix things. They simply move on. That's what privileged men do. Roger Martin, richest kid in your school, took advantage of you. I'm not saying your Danny Manelli is like that. I'm saying be careful."

Relief fluttered through Marnie. "I'm always careful."

Maybe too careful.

The words popped into her brain unbidden. But there was a bitter truth to them. She'd been nothing but careful since high school. Since the pictures. Since the two-year rebellion that had landed her in bed with a predator.

Wasn't it time to forgive herself?

Wasn't it time to step out and have a real life instead of sporadic dates with guys so safe they hadn't made a ripple of reaction in her life?

Her mom huffed out a sigh. "Look at me. Projecting my own insecurities on you."

"You have good reason."

"We both have good reason." She shook her head. "I guess maybe what I'm saying is think this through. The man is your boss. And you might be taking things out of context—"

"I'm being smart. Nothing's really happened." She fought the urge to squeeze her eyes shut. Danny's kiss a few nights ago had been fraught with hunger. Her kiss that very afternoon had been the answer to it.

She wasn't being smart or careful or wise or even prudent.

Her mom was right. She was charging forward on instinct. A need she hadn't felt in years. Which meant she might not know how to control it.

She rose from the chair. "We should make tea and play rummy."

Her mom also stood. "Are you staying!"

"I could. But I probably shouldn't. I have Rex on a great schedule. I'd like to keep that going."

"Okay. We'll play one game or two, then you can get back."

That was the thing she liked best about her mom. She could worry and give warnings, but she trusted Marnie to make good choices and do the right thing.

After two games of rummy, Marnie took public transportation back to Danny's, reminding herself of all the reasons her mom was right. But when she stepped off the elevator and saw Danny coming up the hall from having put Rex to bed, a towel over his shoulder, his shirt askew, his hair a mess, she pressed her lips together.

Everything she felt for him rose and bloomed. She couldn't even look at him without her heart thundering.

What she felt for him was right. If she shoved away her fears and only examined his behavior, he was the best man she'd ever known.

And she wanted him. Wanted everything.

She didn't want to be afraid anymore.

Danny saw Marnie step off the elevator and stopped dead in his tracks. Their eyes met and she started walking toward him. She was the most naturally beautiful woman he'd ever met. Good with his son. Good with him. Good *for* him.

Maybe Leni had been right? Maybe his suspicions were only his fear of making a mistake, holding him back when he longed to go forward. Alisha hadn't been honest with him. His parents hadn't been honest with him. Mark had made him look like an idiot, giving him the job as attorney for his estate then faking his death.

No wonder he feared. But there was no reason to doubt himself, his instincts. Everything that made him suspicious had resulted from the behavior of someone else.

Not him…

Not his choices.

Not his decisions.

And when he looked at Marnie, all his concerns melted away. He was himself again. Because she was honest. Kind. Wonderful.

He took a step, then another, then another, and before he really understood what was going on, they were running to each other. They met in a blistering kiss. Arousal poured through him like the hard rains of a hurricane. Mindless, ravenous, he reached for her top as she plucked his shirt out of his pants.

Two seconds before they would have been naked, common sense hit. "Not here." He barely raised his lips above hers. "There are too many people the doorman is authorized to give the elevator code to." He walked backward toward his room, kicked open the door and led her to the bed.

They fell to the mattress and he rolled her once so that he was on top and could kiss her with all his pent-up need. Their tongues dueled. She rippled her fingers over his naked chest and his muscles hardened.

The kiss turned rough, desperate. He maneuvered them until she was on top and he could run his hands along her torso, her hips, her breasts. Her sharp intake of breath had him pulling her down, giving his tongue access to her soft flesh.

Frenzied need drove him. There would be time to be gentle, patient, later. Once the hunger was assuaged. Limbs tangled. Desire spiked, compelled. Their bodies moved in unison until they finally joined.

A sense of rightness nearly overwhelmed him. The word *mine* whispered through his soul. The notion that he'd spent his entire life looking for her urged him on until completion took them both. Then his breath stilled. His body calmed. His mind quieted until only one thought remained.

He hoped he hadn't made a mistake.

He rose up, caught her gaze—

She smiled. He smiled. His confusion flitted away. Looking at her, being with her, everything in his world righted.

CHAPTER ELEVEN

MARNIE COULDN'T TAKE her eyes off him. Her first sexual experience had been tainted by the pictures. Her subsequent experiences had been tame, careful. Making love with Danny had been explosive and powerful. Not just sexually, but emotionally. Everything they felt had been right there, in everything they'd done. Every move. Every taste. Every breath of longing.

Her eyes locked with his, she whispered, "That was amazing."

"Totally." His answering whisper, filled with the same awe, made her smile.

He rolled to his back, his arms around her waist so he could pull her with him, and she cuddled into his side. She wanted to lay her head on his chest, but despite her boldness while they were making love, she couldn't quite bring herself to do it. She settled for letting her hands drift along the hard muscles, ease through the dark hair, luxuriate in the feel of the firm skin beneath her fingertips.

Nothing had ever felt so right. So perfect, but also so normal. As if this was where she was meant to be.

The thought should have scared her. Instead it filled her with wonderment. She hadn't trusted anybody like this in decades.

"We should go out sometime."

Danny's out-of-the-blue comment made her laugh and sit up so she could see his face. "What?"

"We should go out."

She held back a laugh. "Like on a date?"

"It is customary for people who like each other to do that."

She swirled her index finger along his chest. "We did go out…once."

"So now we'll go out again. Maybe dinner."

"Charlotte likes to babysit."

He snickered. "No kidding. I have no idea what's gotten into her. You know, she used to run the operations division of a development company." He shook his head. "Money makes people do crazy things."

"Or maybe it makes them do the things they've wanted all along but just never realized."

He sniffed.

"What have you always wanted to do?"

He met her gaze. "Exactly what I'm doing now."

Pleasure rippled through her. She couldn't tell if he meant being a lawyer or lying here with her, but her heart had taken it that he wanted to be with her.

"I'm serious. Is there nothing you want? Nothing you'd change?"

He took a long breath. "There is one thing that was perfect but got screwed up when Mark announced I was his third kid."

"What's that?"

"I have no idea how to fix things with my adoptive parents. I moved to New York City to find a great job. Not just a good job, a great one." His hand drifted up her side from hip to waist and back down again to settle on the curve. "Once I landed at Waters, Waters and Montgomery, Mark began bringing work to them until they had pretty much taken over all his legal matters."

"What's that have to do with your parents?"

He shook his head. "It's just another piece of distance between us. Another way Mark edged in, taking their place."

Pride shimmied through her and an emotion so deep and fierce she couldn't name it. The way he trusted her with the facts of his life all but cemented their feelings for each other. The way he wanted her advice made her long to be wise enough to help him.

Finally, she said, "Leni was adopted. How did she reconcile that?"

"She and Nick live in her small town in Kansas. Mark is the visitor into her life. Her parents are still her parents. Mark is the guest."

"So maybe you need to think of a way to do that too?"

His eyebrows angled together. "Bring my parents here?"

"Or get a house near them."

"I'd have to commute to work."

She laughed. "Oh, silly man. Don't you know rich guys have weekend homes? Houses in the country?"

He frowned. "That's true."

"And wouldn't you love giving Rex and Wiggles time in the small town you grew up in?"

He laughed. "Yes."

"So the answer is easy."

He rose up, put his hands on her shoulders and maneuvered her down to the pillow again. "Nope. I think the truth is you're brilliant."

Her lips lifted into a smile. "I have been told I'm smart."

He laughed, then kissed her. The simple meeting of their mouths morphing into the scorching need that always ignited between them.

But the sound of the elevator door opening rippled down the hall. Danny had kicked open the master bedroom door and hadn't closed it. Anybody stepping out would have an unobstructed view of the corridor, into his room.

He lifted his head, stifling a groan over being interrupted when he least wanted to be.

The list of people authorized to get that day's code raced through his brain. He jumped off the bed and into his pants. "This could only be one of about seven people." He smiled at her. "Let's hope it's Arnie, the doorman."

She pushed herself up onto her elbows. "I'm guessing that's best-case scenario?"

Yanking a T-shirt over his head, he said, "Yeah. You stay. I'll be right back." Then, unable to help himself, he bent across the bed and brushed a quick kiss across her mouth.

Everything inside him wanted to slam closed the bedroom door and crawl back into bed with her. But one or two of the people who knew the code would have come looking for him. Jace for sure. Charlotte a definite maybe. And Mark—

"Hey, Danny?"

Damn! It was Mark!

Even as he thought that, his father, Mark Hinton and Penny Fillion, his fiancée, peeked down the hall.

He hoped he didn't look like the jumbled mess that he felt.

"Hey…"

He ambled up the corridor, picking up his discarded shirt and rolling it into a ball that he tossed into the guest bathroom, trying to look calm and composed and not like he'd just had desperate sex with a woman he might be falling in love with.

Oh, Mark would love that. He'd give him a sermon on responsibility. Or maybe safe sex—

Oh God! Acting like a real father after thirty years of nothing?

That was the thing about Mark that really rattled him.

"What do you want, Mark?" If his voice came out gruff and angry, so be it. The simple high of having made love to the most beautiful woman he knew evaporated. "You can't just pop into my house."

Even as he said that, he heard a door close behind him. He turned, saw Marnie, fully dressed, walking up the hall. She said, "Rex is asleep." Then seeing Mark and Penny, she smiled. "Hello."

"Marnie, this is my biological father and his fiancée, Penny Fillion." He motioned to tall, slender Mark with white hair now growing on his formerly bald head and short, sweet Penny, who had long yellow hair and bright blue eyes. "Mark, Penny, this is Rex's nanny, Marnie."

To her credit, Marnie casually reached out and shook hands with them both.

"I was just telling Mark that he shouldn't just barge in."

"I'm sorry," Mark said, turning to Marnie. "I apologize if you just got the baby to sleep, but I needed to talk to my son."

The easy way *my son* spilled from Mark's lips sent a crackle of annoyance up Danny's spine. He'd known this man was his father less than three months. Yet Mark behaved as if he'd been around for softball games and soccer practice.

Much kinder than Danny, Marnie smiled. "That's okay."

"Good. Glad I'm not interrupting anything."

Danny's last nerve frayed. "What do you want?"

"Well, I'd hoped to see Rex. But if your nanny put him to bed, I can wait until tomorrow." Mark turned to Marnie. "Isn't that baby adorable?" His brown eyes glowed. "And smart. And I'm not just saying that because he's my grandson. The kid is special. Wonderful." He motioned to Penny. "We're hoping Rex will be ring bearer at our wedding. We're getting married in September."

"In Paris," Penny said dreamily.

Marnie hugged Penny. "That's wonderful."

Mark's smile warmed. "We're here because we decided Danny should be our best man."

Danny's head about exploded. Trying to give his dad the benefit of the doubt, he told himself Mark had simply chosen his words poorly. But… Seriously? He'd *decided* Danny should be his best man? He didn't ask?

Mark glanced over at him. "Will you be our best man?"

Danny's anger deflated a bit. All right. He'd asked. "I don't know, Mark. Everything's different now that I have custody of Rex."

Mark grinned. "That's the beauty of you and Rex both being in the wedding. With you as best man and Rex as ring bearer, you'll be in the same place at the same time."

Danny gaped at him. "He's *two*. I'm not sure he can walk down the aisle on his own yet. Unless you have a flower girl who's willing to hold his hand and drag him to the altar, Rex being ring bearer might not be a good idea."

"Okay. I get that."

Guilt flooded Danny. Mark might be a tornado, but when Danny least expected it, he'd pull back, clearly demonstrating he was trying to get along.

"I'm not saying no. We just have to see what he can do and what he can't."

"I get that too." Mark smiled ruefully. "We're happy to wait for your answer about being best man." Then he turned to Penny. "Ready for cheesecake at Junior's?"

She laughed and looped her arm through his. "That means we eat salads tomorrow."

They headed for the elevator. "You're no fun."

"I'm tons of fun. I simply won't let you eat a totally unhealthy diet."

Marnie wistfully watched them leave, and Danny remembered what they'd been doing before they'd been interrupted. They'd been in the middle of something life changing when Mark had simply walked in.

All the books he'd been reading on raising children said that a person couldn't reward inappropriate behavior. His dad might not be a child, but Danny couldn't let him go on thinking it was okay for him to interrupt him.

"Mark," he called right before the pair entered the elevator.

Mark turned. "Yeah."

"I'm serious about coming up to the penthouse without letting me know. You need to respect my time and call before dropping in. Otherwise, I'll have Jace change the locks and instruct the doorman that you're *never* to be let up."

Danny's words came out harsher than he'd intended, but Mark laughed. "You should come work for Hinton, then I could see you at the office."

And wouldn't that be peachy? Him, working for a man he wasn't even sure he liked. Having him pop into his office when he was knee-deep in reading a contract. "I love my current job. I don't want another."

Mark batted a hand. "You'll come around."

Marnie watched as Mark and Penny stepped in the plush car that would take them back to the lobby. But it wasn't empty. The guy from the park, the one who'd rescued Wiggles from the bush, stood along the back wall, dressed in a suit with a wire coming out of his ear.

Pretty Penny waved goodbye. Mark saluted. Danny sighed. The elevator doors closed, and the car headed down.

"Who was the guy in the elevator?"

Danny faced Marnie. "What guy?"

"Blue suit, white shirt? Receiver in his ear—" Everything came together in her brain. "Like a bodyguard."

"Oh, you mean Bruce! That *is* a bodyguard. He's one of about twenty guys who discreetly follow us around."

"He's the guy who pulled Wiggles from the bush."

Danny shrugged and headed for the kitchen. "It must have been his day to guard Rex."

Gobsmacked, she fell into one of the paisley chairs. "Guard Rex? There's someone been guarding Rex the whole time I've worked for you and you didn't tell me?"

He pulled the fixings for a sandwich out of the refrigerator. "Of course, I told you."

"No! You didn't! Dear God, Danny, I would have remembered something like that."

"Marnie, when I interviewed you, I said something about how my life was different. I know I mentioned bodyguards."

"You dropped it into the conversation. You didn't explain that I'd actually have one. You didn't tell me to look for one or how to deal with one."

"Because there's nothing for you to do. They

are in the background, discreet. They're not supposed to be a part of your world. They're only watching."

Disbelief trembled through her. "For weeks I've had someone following me around?" It might not have been as bad as a boyfriend taking naked pictures, but it felt like an intrusion, a betrayal, that she hadn't been told.

"No. If you'd taken the limo to your mom's, you would have had someone following you around. Or shopping the other Saturday. The bodyguard is the driver. When you have the baby outside for a walk, *Rex* has someone following *him*." He took a breath. "My dad is a couple billion away from being a trillionaire. His grandson could easily be snatched for ransom."

She shook her head, confusion hardening her voice. "It still feels like a betrayal. If I look at this the right way, I could think you were spying on me."

He dropped his sandwich to the island. "How can you think that?"

"How do I know you're not getting a report every night?"

"Of what?"

"Of what I did that day."

"They never come into the penthouse unless I

ask them to. Most are drivers. When they aren't taking Rex somewhere or following Rex on a walk, they sit in the car, watching the building. They know who comes and goes. Know the postmen."

She stared at him. "That sounds a hell of a lot like a prison."

He combed his fingers through his hair. It had taken him weeks to get accustomed to all this, to find his footing, to accept it. And with a few words, she threatened to undermine it.

"It's all in how you look at it. I do exactly as I want. They are the ones who scramble to keep up with me."

Her eyebrows rose.

"I'm not sure what your beef is. You should be glad Rex is being protected. You are his nanny. His caregiver."

She rose. "Yeah. I guess that's true. As Rex's *nanny* I don't have rights. I don't have a say in the big picture." She cleared her throat. "I don't know what got into me thinking I was more."

She turned and headed down the hall to her room, and Danny groaned. "Marnie…wait! I'm sorry. It's like we're arguing two different things."

She stopped. Faced him. "Oh, don't worry. I

won't be like one of your families fighting over an estate. I won't dig in my heels and try to get something I don't deserve. I *know* I have no rights."

With that, she turned and walked back to her room. Part of Danny ached to follow her. But it was getting Rex that had made him see the necessity of high security and bodyguards—

Though bodyguards really weren't the issue. It was that he hadn't told her. Meeting her dad in the park, he realized she had trust issues and why. And she was justifiably angry tonight. He'd thought he'd told her about the bodyguards and assumed she'd know that included Rex. But he didn't want to argue and end up making concessions he shouldn't make because of what had happened in his bedroom.

He thought about making love. How passionate and happy they were. How all that perfection had disappeared because she had issues too. His trust issues might be fresher, but hers had had time to fester.

He sank to the sofa and put his forehead in his hands, refusing to panic. Tomorrow they'd both be in a better frame of mind. A little sleep and some distance would put it all into focus and they could talk like normal people.

But tonight, he wouldn't have the pleasure of holding her until they both fell asleep. They wouldn't make love again, slowly. He wouldn't get to leisurely explore her curves or sink into her soft skin.

He shook his head, forced his brain to stop. He'd thought he and Leni had talked out his suspicions, but the thing he hadn't mentioned was his feelings for Marnie. Too fast. Too deep. Too much.

Maybe it was good they were stepping back?

CHAPTER TWELVE

MARNIE HAD REX in the highchair when Danny came into the kitchen the next morning. Their gazes met and she quickly looked away. She knew he didn't understand why she'd gotten so angry the night before.

He walked to the coffeemaker. "Good morning."

"Good morning."

He busied himself with closing a pod in the holder and putting a cup under the drip. "If you go out today, a bodyguard will be watching Rex."

She shook her head. "I know. I'm sorry. I thought about it last night and realized a kid with a near trillionaire for a granddad would need security."

"But that really wasn't the issue, was it? It was trust. I thought you understood what I meant when I talked about bodyguards in your interview, and you didn't fully get it. So you felt like I'd kept something from you."

"I'm not sure what I felt."

"Marnie, your dad is a louse. Not to mention that you probably had some bad times when you were a kid, before your mom went to A.A."

She licked her lips.

"I get it."

"You shouldn't have to get it. I'm a professional. Our...personal stuff is making me act differently than I normally would."

"I get that too."

She dragged in a breath. Every second of what they'd done the day before played through her brain. The wonderful pleasure. The closeness she'd never had. Her realization that she couldn't have it. She couldn't drag him into her craziness. Not when he had his own things to deal with.

"Please, stop being so understanding. I'm a mess. Not someone a smart man has a relationship with."

His eyes softened. "Marnie..."

"Stop. Really. This is why I don't date a lot. I'm not crazy. I just had some things happen to me that make me so paranoid that I react oddly about normal things. Get suspicious over things I shouldn't."

He sniffed a laughed. "I just had this same conversation with my sister Leni yesterday while you were gone. She'd made cookies for Rex, and I ended up telling her that I had worried that you'd only wanted to work for me to get access to your dad."

Surprise poured through her. She didn't know why she'd thought he'd fallen into their relationship without thinking. The fact that he hadn't made her feel the tiniest bit better.

"No. I'm not exactly a fan of my dad. Seeing him threw me." She laughed unexpectedly. "Had I known I had a bodyguard I might have confronted him myself, sooner."

"Good. See? We're at the stage where we can laugh about the bodyguard."

She rolled her eyes. When she'd woken that morning, she'd been so sure they'd made a mistake. Now, calmer, she didn't know what to think.

"My point, though, is that I've got some unusual stuff in my life too. I love my parents with every fiber of my being, but the fact that they never told me I was adopted broke trust."

"I can see how that would happen."

"Then my biological dad storms into my life because he's found out I have a child."

"How'd he do that?"

"A private investigator apparently took note of new people in my life and occasionally checked

on them. He found Rex, did some math and confronted Alisha."

"Wow."

"In one big swoop, I discovered I was adopted,
had a child and had a dad who'd literally been
spying on me my whole life."

"Makes a bodyguard look insignificant."

"Yes, it does." He added cream to his coffee and
walked it to the center island. "Still, that doesn't
make what happened to you insignificant."

She sniffed. She loved that he was so understanding, but he didn't know her real pain. She
hadn't told him her secret.

Her past came back in a wave of memories. She
wanted to tell him. Longed to tell him. But the
humiliation of it froze the words in her throat.

"Marnie?"

Her gaze jumped to his.

"Come on. We're both coming clean. Our cir-
cumstance is unique. If we really want to have
something, we can't have secrets."

She squeezed her eyes shut. "We can't have
something."

"Because of a little misstep about a bodyguard?"

She shook her head. "I was bullied at school. I
erased my social media profiles, changed schools,

took my mother's maiden name and in a weird kind of way, disappeared. If you search me, it's like the beginning part of my life didn't exist."

His mouth dropped open and he snapped it shut, thinking for a few seconds before he said, "You must have been bullied pretty badly."

"I was." She took a breath, surprised at the sense of a weight being lifted off her shoulders. "Actually, it's sort of a relief to tell you. Now I don't have to look like an idiot walking away from something good. Something I want."

His eyes darkened. "Why does being bullied at school make you feel you have to walk away?"

"I was bullied because my mother called the police on a jock who'd taken pictures of me after… we…" She closed her eyes, sucked in a breath. "My first years in high school, I was kind of a tease. The boys had this bet going about who'd get my virginity. I didn't know anything about it. I fell for the jock, and after we'd done it, he took pictures as proof. He showed them around to the boys at school, then offered them for sale."

"Oh my God." Danny looked so shocked that she almost felt sorry for him.

"When I found out, I raced home and told my mom. She called the police, who came to the school. They made him delete the pictures from his phone." She stopped, caught his gaze. "But I don't really know that they were destroyed. He could have them somewhere, like an old thumb drive." She sucked in a breath. "I can't date you. I shouldn't even be seen in public with you. Someday somebody's going to get interested or curious and a good reporter will do a thorough search and piece it all together. Then it'll come out—my association with someone so newsworthy will make it a headline instead of an article buried in the newspaper. And I'll go through it all again. The humiliation. The feeling that I'm worthless. Nothing. Just someone to be abused."

He held her gaze for a few minutes. His sympathy for her right there in his dark orbs. She hated it. All she'd ever wanted was to be normal and it seemed life couldn't let her have that.

He set his coffee on the island. "Let me look up the law, see if there's anything we can do… Times have changed, Marnie. And the statute might not have run out."

She put her hand on his forearm, her heart in her throat. The memories of the episode that had destroyed her life riffled through her brain. Humiliation rose and cut deep. Typical fears for her future raced through her.

"Oh my God. Don't you see? That's what I

don't want. I don't want one of the richest men in the world going after him. The press would have a field day. And I'd be front and center in every newspaper in the country." She sucked in a breath. "I just want to be left alone. And maybe someday start a little company and live a quiet life."

She caught his gaze, her eyes filled with a misery that somehow held a glimmer of hope, and Danny's heart shattered. All these weeks he'd been feeling sorry for himself for discovering his parents weren't his biological parents and his actual dad was an eccentric billionaire. While Marnie had real troubles. Real problems. A real ache from her past that could explode into her present.

He wanted to kick himself for being so selfish. So self-absorbed.

He reached for her hand. "How does a person come back from something like that?" He wanted to say, "How does a *kid* come back from something like that," because she couldn't have been more than a teenager when it happened, but he thought better of it.

She shrugged. "My mom was pretty smart. My father owns one of the biggest real estate companies in New York State. He left her and ultimately had us evicted from our condo because only his name was on the deed. He has so many friends in high places that she got virtually no child support for me until she found a lawyer willing to dig really deep into his finances. She can hold her own."

"Smart woman."

She sniffed a laugh, pulled her hand from Danny's and rose. "Yeah. She learned some hard lessons." She headed back down the hall again. "I'll go pack and call Shirley. It's Sunday, but she can still have someone here in a couple of hours. I'll stay until the new nanny arrives."

His heart stopped. Something strong and angry rose in him. He might be part of a family that needed protecting, but he couldn't deny this woman a job she so clearly deserved. "You don't have to leave."

She stopped and returned to the kitchen. "Have you ever thought of what your future brother-in-law would do if he heard my story? You say your dad's biggest worry is of one of you being kidnapped… What about extortion? Roger hasn't been a blip on the radar of my life for a decade. But what if there's a picture of us in the paper when we're walking Wiggles? What if he comes out of the woodwork? If Jace finds out about my past, that's what he's going to consider. Extortion. If Roger comes after me, asking for money, your father's estate wouldn't have to do a thing. Once they fired me, they'd be free. I'm the one who'd be picking up those pieces."

She shook her head. "I'd sort of thought of all of this as I was packing to work here. On the train, I'd decided not to take the job. But then I got out of the elevator, and Rex was crying, milk was everywhere...and you were so nice." Tears filled her eyes. "I just wanted to help you."

"You are helping, Marnie. Your secret's stayed a secret for ten years. It may never come up again."

She wavered. He saw it in her eyes, and something compelled him to persuade her. Maybe he wanted to return everything life had taken away from her. Maybe he simply couldn't stand to see her so hurt, so empty, when she deserved the world.

"Stay." He reached out and squeezed her hand. "Rex loves you. I need you. You could leave now, but what if you stay and nothing happens?"

She worried her bottom lip.

"Stay."

She raised her eyes until their gazes caught. "If I stay, there can't be anything between us. Seeing the bodyguard, realizing just how rich and different you are, it hit me in a wave that anything between you and me would be a nightmare. You have to promise there will be nothing between us."

He thought of everything that had happened the day before. Thought of confronting her dad. Marnie kissing him. The suspicions that had rolled over him like a freight train. His chat with Leni and how in the end, no matter that he'd had suspicions, he hadn't been able to resist Marnie.

He said, "I promise," but something inside him told him it was a lie. He'd never felt the things he felt for her. Sometimes they drew him along before he had a chance to really think them through.

Still, after everything she'd endured in her very young life, he couldn't be the one to put her through anything more.

Especially not for something as trivial as a romance...

The thought died in his brain. What he felt for her, with her, wasn't trivial.

And maybe that was the problem.

For the next week, every day when Danny went to work, the temptation to search the name of the guy who had ruined Marnie's life nearly overwhelmed him, but he didn't even open his browser. He reminded himself that Marnie didn't want her secrets unburied. The irony of it rolled through him as he turned to look out the wall of glass behind his desk.

The man whose life had been undone by secrets had fallen for a woman whose secret could destroy her.

Which led him to realize that maybe the real issue wasn't that there were pictures potentially out there, but her fear of them.

He returned home that night tired, worn down, but the second he saw her, sitting in front of the highchair feeding Rex, his spirit rose.

"Hey! Hi, everybody." He walked from the elevator to the island, where he set his briefcase. He reached for the spoon to give Rex his next bite and Marnie melted back, away from him. He told himself it was to let him have special time with Rex and turned his attention to his son.

"So how was your day?"

Rex giggled and said, "Good."

"Today's bodyguard, Paul, took him for a nice, long walk."

His chest tightened. "Did you not want to go?"

"No." She busied herself at the sink. "I just thought I'd eliminate the middleman. Let Rex go out and the bodyguard have total control."

"You don't have to do that."

"I know."

"You don't want to go outside?"

She hesitated. "I'm fine inside."

Where no one could see her. Especially not with his child.

His little boy finished eating and Danny unstrapped him from the highchair and pulled him into his arms.

Marnie raced over. "Don't forget his juice. He didn't drink a lot today, so I'm encouraging fluids."

He turned to take the cup from her. Their hands brushed and a million sensations roared through him. Enough that his breath caught.

Their eyes met and she blinked, but not before he saw the shimmer of longing that she banked.

"I should probably go to my room. Let you have some playtime before he goes to bed."

His soul shattered into a million pieces. He wanted to hold her, to make it better. To take her to his bed and love her until nothing else mattered. But her walls were solid, and he understood why.

Still, they were on the top floor of an exclusive building. With a doorman and bodyguards and no one to see…

"Why not play with us?"

She smiled slightly. "Because he needs time alone with you. Not just with me."

"You love playing with us. Rex loves when we all play together—"

"True, but it's been a long day. I'll just go get a shower."

Disappointment gripped him. His pride bruised. He stepped back. "Yeah. Sure."

He left the kitchen and took Rex to the nursery, where he entertained his son so long that he got him ready for bed.

Marnie tiptoed in. "You didn't have to do that. I would have helped."

"It's okay." He'd fought off the injury to his pride with cold, hard facts. He knew he didn't understand anything she felt. He'd tried to imagine the horrible betrayal she'd gone through, but how could he get the full impact of something like that? He couldn't. He thought about what she'd said about extortion and what Jace would say if he knew, and he honestly didn't have any answers. Particularly when he remembered the revelation of Mark's secrets had ruined his life. Changed it so much he would never be the same again.

That's what outing Marnie's secrets would do to her.

No matter how much it hurt him, confused him, filled him with longing that morphed into anger sometimes, he thought of her.

He said, "Good night," and retreated to his room, walking to the window.

He could buy anything he saw. Fancy cars. Fancy meals. Fancy clothes. Even a whole damned building. But the one thing he really wanted he couldn't have.

Anger lit in his soul. A fight between the part of him that understood that she had to be careful and the part of him that wanted her to let go.

Test the waters. See if there really was a reason to be worried.

But it only took asking her to go for a walk with him and Rex on Saturday morning for him to see the genuine fear in her eyes.

It made him crazy and his heart ached for her, but he also missed her. He hated that he was the cause of her withdrawal, then he'd think about how happy they'd been. Even before their feelings for each other had pulled them into something she didn't want, they'd been happy.

He'd been even more contented than he'd been before he'd discovered he was the son of an eccentric billionaire. It was as if being with her made everything in his life unimportant, except her and Rex. Those were his priorities and his joy. And he knew he'd been changing her feelings, her life too.

They'd both fallen into something wonderful, and now it was gone.

Monday morning, his phone office phone buzzed, and he hit the button to answer. "Yes."

"It's Monty. Your sister Charlotte and her fiancé are on their way up."

Normally, a visit from Charlotte and Jace would have been a welcome announcement. He loved Charlotte. Quick-witted and smart, she always made him laugh. But she had Jace with her. And, after Marnie's story, anytime anyone mentioned Jace, Danny stiffened.

What if Jace had investigated her?

What if Jace had uncovered her secret?

Was he here to tell Danny he had to fire her? After all, the Hinton family didn't take chances. Jace axed anything that could potentially lead to trouble.

The elevator door opened. Charlotte strode out. Wearing dress slacks and a silky tank top and blazer, she looked like she'd been born to money. In his black suit and tie, Jace was clearly her match.

As Danny rose, she walked to the desk and planted a big kiss on his cheek.

"You're in a good mood."

Jace said, "We have news."

Danny's heart stumbled at the possibilities. But would Charlotte be so chipper if Jace had uncovered Marnie's secret and they were here to force him to fire her?

No. She wouldn't.

They couldn't know.

He motioned for them to take the seats in front of his desk.

"What's up?"

"I'm pregnant!" Charlotte said without preamble, clearly so happy she was ready to burst.

Jace shook his head. "She's nuts about it."

"Are you kidding? A little Jace!" Her face glowed. "What could be cuter than that?"

Danny laughed and rose, coming around the desk to shake Jace's hand and hug Charlotte. "Congratulations!"

"That's not the best news," Charlotte said. "We're getting married next week—in *Scotland*!"

"Next week?"

"In *Scotland!*"

He laughed. "Yeah. I got that part."

"Why aren't you jumping for joy?"

He shook his head. "Now that I'm a dad, there are logistics to think about."

Charlotte blinked. "You are bringing Rex, right?"

"Of course."

Jace gave him a funny look. "And you have a nanny."

"Right."

"See?" Charlotte pointed her finger at him. "That right there. That's what lawyers do. Make a big deal out of things that don't need to be a big deal."

His head tilted. "What?"

"Danny, when we thought Mark was dead, you made a production number out of everything that had to do with his estate. You did three DNA samples on me and Leni and sent them to three different labs. You kept Leni locked away in a hotel room and tried to stifle me, but I'm not so easily corralled."

Jace nodded. "It's true."

"And now you're making a production number out of going to Scotland when we have private jets and can stay anywhere we want. For once just relax. We're going to Scotland…for a *wedding.* Because Jace and I are going to have a *baby.*" She glanced at Jace. "Our own little bundle of joy. Don't pick it apart. Don't ask yourself if you're being too happy. Just come with us to Scotland, dance a bit, drink as much as you want and let go."

He stared at her.

She chuckled and rose from her seat. "I know the concept of relaxing eludes you. But try it—for me." She patted her stomach. "For us." She glanced at Jace again. "For all of us. Maybe it's time we stopped second-guessing things about our new lives and were happy. Stop picking until we find the dark cloud that we can hide under."

Danny blinked, watching them leave. They'd said goodbye, but he'd been preoccupied with what Charlotte had said.

Did he really pick everything apart until he found the dark cloud?

And was that what Marnie was doing. So afraid of being hurt, she kept her dark cloud front and center?

Let it guide her life?

Let it *ruin* her life?

CHAPTER THIRTEEN

MARNIE HAD JUST finished giving Rex a bath after feeding him spaghetti for dinner, when Danny arrived home. He dropped his briefcase on the center island and took Rex from her arms, then kissed his forehead.

"I ordered Chinese for dinner. It should be here any minute."

She backed away. Several days had gone by with her keeping her distance. She had finally adjusted, and she didn't want anything to happen to bring back the sadness that had threatened to suffocate her when they'd stopped talking.

For at least six of the first seven days, she'd ached the whole way to her bones. Not because she liked him, but because he liked her. Just as she was. They could talk about anything. They understood each other... And making love? She'd never experienced that kind of fire, tempered by the sweetness of the emotion they felt for each other.

Thinking about it now filled her chest with

such longing her breath hitched and her voice stuttered when she said, "That's okay. I can make a sandwich."

"You can't live on sandwiches. Besides, we have something to talk about."

Her gaze leaped to his. "We do?"

Before she could jump to myriad conclusions that would have paralyzed her, he said, "Yes. Charlotte and Jace are getting married."

Relief made her weak, but happiness for Charlotte and Jace superseded that. "Well, of course, they are. They're engaged."

He slid Rex into his highchair, buckled him in. "No. I don't mean they're getting married in general. I mean they're getting married next week. In Scotland."

Her mouth dropped open. "Oh my gosh! That's so cool."

"She's pregnant, thrilled and running on adrenaline."

She laughed, picturing already-energetic Charlotte running on adrenaline. "I'm so happy for her!"

The elevator pinged and the doorman stepped out carrying two bags. "Your food is here."

Danny took it from him. "Thanks."

He winked at Marnie and was gone.

Forgetting she was supposed to keep her distance, she said, "The doormen love you, even though I've never seen you tip even one of them."

Danny brought the Chinese to the center island. "Every month my father gives each of them a couple thousand dollars to take care of tips." He rooted through a bag and brought out a container with a metal handle. "I raised it another thousand."

A laugh bubbled up, even though she didn't want it to. But this was what always happened when they spent time together. They laughed. They talked. They connected.

She took two plates out of the cabinet and brought them to the table. They couldn't help it. They clicked. But maybe instead of fighting it, she should redirect it, temper it. They couldn't very well go on not talking. Discussing something as neutral as him tipping the doormen was a safe way to ease them into a normal nanny/employer relationship. Maybe if they could talk without getting personal, she'd get her bearings and the yearning in her heart would go away.

"You stacked the deck."

"Not really." He pulled out a container of egg rolls. "I just wanted to distinguish myself from my father. This isn't really my penthouse. I'm only using it." He paused, seemed to think about something, then said, "From what I know of the family holdings, no one actually owns anything. It's all owned by a Hinton shell company. We simply have access to anything we want. Anytime we want."

One of Marnie's eyebrows rose. To a person who'd rented her entire life, owning a home was a dream. The American Dream. She couldn't wrap her head around having access to everything and owning nothing—

"That's weird."

He caught her gaze, clearly surprised she'd continued the conversation. "It takes a while to get used to."

She filled a plate and walked around to the stools, sitting on the first one, determined to get them back to solid ground by talking about something so neutral it didn't matter.

"You can go anywhere you want, anytime you want?"

"We have access to planes. Big planes. Small planes. Jets." He finished filling his dish and sat beside her. "Mark owns two islands."

She gaped at him. "Are you kidding?"

"And something like twenty-six houses, including condos in Barcelona and Paris."

"He has a condo in Paris?"

"It's probably more like a penthouse." He took a breath. "There are boats, Jet Skis, houses in places like Aspen. There's a ranch in Canada and one in Texas. And he's mentioned buying one in Montana."

"Wow."

They fell silent as they both dug into their food, and Rex amused himself with a small bear. Her father and Roger Martin's father were paupers compared to Mark Hinton.

"The point is, we can use anything he owns anytime we want."

"What if somebody else is already there?"

"Leni's Nick employs three people who do nothing but track the properties, insure them, maintain them. They have a schedule."

She shook her head. "It boggles the mind."

"You should be me, Leni or Charlotte, three only children, raised in solidly middle-class families. Charlotte, I think, adjusted the best because she had a sense of humor about it. Leni adjusted because she's kind. Generous. Sweet. She wants the world to get along. She walks the walk."

Marnie glanced over at him. "And what about you?"

He shrugged. "Are you sure you want to hear this? We'd sort of made a pact not to be friends."

"Making a pact doesn't mean I stopped liking you, being interested in your life. I'm trying to get us to a normal place where we can talk as boss and employee and not be miserable all the time."

"I don't want you to be uncomfortable. But I haven't stopped liking you either. You were the balance that I needed. Someone to care for Rex who was easy to talk to."

And she'd loved that. Loved that he needed her as much as liked her. With him, she'd felt as if she'd found a place, a home. Not four walls and a bed, but a niche that warmed her, gave her a sense of self and independence she'd never had before. Particularly since he'd needed her and enjoyed her company as much as she'd needed a home, a space to be herself.

He shrugged. "Telling me I'm not allowed to like you is equivalent to telling the sun not to rise."

She knew exactly what he meant. Her feelings were too easy, too genuine. She'd had to retreat to her room every night for the past few days to keep them from overwhelming her. Even now, just talking to him, had warmed her heart.

"So, to get back to the point… We're going to Scotland with you as Rex's nanny."

Gobsmacked, she pressed her hand to her chest "*I'm* going to Scotland?"

"Rex is invited to every party and celebration, but he still has a bedtime, needs to be fed on a schedule…"

"*I'm going to Scotland?*"

He laughed. "Your enthusiasm reminds me of Charlotte's."

"I don't care if I'm seeing the country with Rex on my hip, I still get to see Scotland!" She bounced from her stool. "I need to buy a few things."

His head tilted. "Like what?"

"I'm not running around Scotland in yoga pants and T-shirts. Actually, I'll need to Google the weather to make sure we pack appropriately for Rex too." She tapped a finger on her lips. "So many things to do." She glanced at Danny. "What day is this wedding?"

"Next Friday. But we're leaving Tuesday."

"Okay. Four days is good. Plenty of time to get everything together."

With that, she raced back to her room, and Danny watched her go. Her delight at going to Scotland filled him with a pleasure that swelled his chest. It was almost as if her joy gave him permission to be excited. Charlotte wanted everyone to stop trying to figure things out and just be happy? Well, that's what Marnie did for him. She grounded him. Maybe because they were raised in a similar way. But whatever the reason, he was so glad he could take her to Scotland, show her the country, enjoy the week of Charlotte's wedding celebration.

He cleaned up their dishes and put away the leftover food, talking to Rex. "What about you? Do you want to see Scotland?"

He giggled.

But a reality he'd thought he understood hit him hard, harder than it ever had. His two-year-old son was about to become a world traveler. In a few years, he'd attend the finest private schools. Go to any university he wanted, anywhere in the world.

"You'll grow up so different than how I did."

Being wealthy had wiped out any financial worry Danny might ever have, but what no one realized was it added an even bigger worry.

How did one lead a normal life with access to anything and everything they wanted? Harder still, how could he possibly raise Rex to be a normal kid when his life would be anything but normal?

The kitchen cleared, he took Rex back to the nursery, read him two stories and put him to bed. When he came out, Marnie was nowhere around. But that didn't surprise him. She had worked to level them off, re-create a normal employer/employee relationship. And now she'd retreat before they took it too far.

He respected that. But his big penthouse was empty and lonely once Rex was in bed. It hadn't been before Marnie came. It had been a normal home to him. Then she'd entered his world and made everything fun. He wouldn't lie to himself and pretend it wasn't her loss that made him lonely. He wanted her. *Her.*

But she hated all the trappings of his new life. And he accepted that.

He went to the family room to play pool, hoping to entice her out of her suite for another game.

But she stayed in her room. Probably looking up the weather in Scotland. He almost knocked on her door to join her to share the fun of the preliminary research before a trip across the Atlantic. But he knew her fears.

And having her eat with him, albeit in a limited way, was better than nothing… Wasn't it?

CHAPTER FOURTEEN

As they approached Scotland, Marnie pointed at the little islands in front of the mainland, then the mountains and green fields separated by trees.

"See, Rex? Isn't it beautiful?"

He said, "Yeth," but squirmed in her arms.

"Come on," Danny said, gesturing for Marnie to hand him over. "Let me get him in his car seat and buckled in. We'll be landing soon."

Marnie helped secure Rex, then took the seat beside him. "Just in case," she said, but Danny shook his head.

"He's fine."

"You never know."

He sat across from them in a little conversation grouping that was both convenient and cozy. The plane landed and she hopped up to get Rex out of his seat.

"I know you're excited, but the door won't open for five or ten minutes. There are checks the pilots have to make."

She said, "That's okay."

Danny took Rex from her. "Look over there," he said, leaning down beside the window, pointing beyond the private airstrip to the countryside. "Uncle Jace's family lives out there."

Rex grinned.

Marnie slid the strap of her duffel bag up her arm. "It was gorgeous from the air."

"Charlotte said it's the most beautiful place she's ever seen. She called it enchanted. I can't wait to see it."

She frowned. "You've never been to Scotland?"

He pointed at his chest. "Middle class, remember?"

"Yeah."

They spent the short trip to the MacDonald compound pointing out scenery to Rex. He really didn't understand, but Danny enjoyed it. A sense of contentment blanketed him. He wasn't working. He wasn't at home with someone whose company he enjoyed, having her ignore him. They were in Scotland, about to celebrate his sister's wedding and Marnie was being herself.

"What are you smiling at?"

"I'm think I'm tapping into what Charlotte feels. I'm happy for her."

"I am too. She and Jace are a great couple and she obviously wants kids."

"That she does."

The limo pulled into the compound into a sea of limos.

"Wow. So, this is what it looks like when the rich get together." She shook her head. "This is going to be a logistical nightmare for Jace's people."

He wondered if she realized how well she knew his family, how she fit. "His upper echelon staff is top-notch. They'll have this area cleared in minutes."

They exited the limo, leaving luggage duties to the driver and the staff Jace had on hand. The huge stone house welcomed them. A carriage house beside it was both quaint and homey. Trees dotted the property. Enough to provide shade and beauty, but not so many that there was no lawn. Green grass flourished between gardens filled with colorful flowers.

The wide-plank front door actually had a crest and a little plaid.

"Look at that," Marnie said, reverently tracing the brass crest. "It must be fun to be Scottish."

Having been given instructions to enter without knocking, they walked into the high-ceilinged foyer. The sound of conversation and laughter filled the air.

Carrying Rex, Danny headed to the kitchen. "We're here!"

Charlotte pushed away from the counter and raced over to give him and Marnie a hug before she kissed Rex's cheek and stole him from his father. "Here's my little love."

Mark was by her side in seconds. "You see him all the time. I've been in Paris buried in wedding details. I hold him first."

They sounded so much like a normal family that a wave of belonging washed over Danny. His adoptive parents rose from the table and walked over too. His mom hugged him. His dad shook his hand, then did a shoulder bump.

"Do we have to take a number to get to hold our own grandson?"

Danny laughed. "I didn't know you guys were coming."

"Of course, they were coming," Charlotte said, sounded affronted. "We have the biggest, weirdest family on the planet, but we are all family."

The truth of that trickled through him. No one wanted him to desert his adoptive parents. He was the one who was having trouble adjusting.

He thought of Marnie's plan for him to get a house in his hometown and he smiled.

Leni's adoptive dad toasted. "To family." A short, stocky construction worker, he'd gone through a surgery and was now project manager on Leni's vision to totally modernize and refurbish her town. Her pretty brunette mom sat beside him.

At the counter, Leni poured champagne as Nick passed it around. Nick's mom and dad were the first to take glasses from the tray.

"Nice to see you, Danny."

"Nice to see you too, Mr. Kourakis."

"Who's your friend?"

Danny winced. "Sorry. This is Marnie Olsen. She's Rex's nanny."

Marnie smiled sweetly, shyly. "Hi, everybody."

"It's lovely to have you here," Nick's mom said. The Kourakis family had had their share of troubles too. An automobile accident killed their younger son. Nick had been driving. His grief had been intense and protracted. There were times Danny had wondered if he'd ever be the same… Then Nick had met Leni.

He glanced at Marnie. Her pink cheeks. Her bright green eyes.

His chest tightened the way it always did when

he looked at her in an unguarded moment. But Nick was suddenly in front of him with the tray of champagne. Charlotte made a joke about not being able to toast at her own wedding celebration because she couldn't drink alcohol while pregnant. Her mom, Penny, beamed with pride. Jace looked rough and rugged in jeans and a plaid shirt. Danny's adoptive parents, Terry and Gene Manelli, laughed with Jace's mom and dad.

And Danny got a picture of the rest of his life. Especially when his mom picked up a plate of hors d'oeuvres and offered one to Marnie, who happily popped the stuffed mushroom into her mouth.

Danny shook his head. "You're going to ruin your dinner. You're *all* going to ruin your dinner."

Someone threw a stuffed mushroom at him. "Who invited this party pooper?"

"I did." Charlotte walked over and slid her arm beneath Danny's. "We're all so crazy. We need a stuffed shirt to keep us in line."

Everybody laughed, but Danny frowned.

He wasn't a stuffed shirt.

Was he?

Was that part of what Charlotte had meant

when she'd told him that he worked to find the dark cloud in everything?

Rex began to fuss, and Marnie edged her way through the crowd in the country kitchen to find him. The toddler fell into her arms, rubbing his eyes.

"Nap time. He snoozed on the plane, but his body knows that every day at two he goes to his crib. It might be evening here, but it's two at home." She smiled at Jace's mom. "Is there some- one who can show us to the room he and Danny will be using?"

Jace came out of the crowd. "Actually, you're not in the house. You're in the suite above the carriage house. There's a room for you and one for Danny large enough to put the crib in. It's the biggest, quietest space we have to make sure Rex isn't disturbed." He winced. "Unfortunately, you have to share a bathroom."

Danny said, "That's fine."

But Marnie's heart skipped a beat. She'd never been in a house packed with so many people be- fore, all of whom thought they were funny. In fairness, most were. Still, her overriding impres- sion was of three unique families, blending into one big family with Mark Hinton as patriarch.

She tried to imagine her dad doing something like this, and when she couldn't she suddenly liked Mark Hinton. What he'd done to bring his family together, including adoptive parents and in-laws was remarkable.

Jace's dad walked to the kitchen door with her, having said he'd show her to the carriage house, but Danny unexpectedly joined them.

"I'm fine. I can get Rex to sleep. You go. Enjoy your family."

He gave her a strange look. Something she hadn't ever seen from him. She thought that he might not want to be with his family, but as they walked out the door he said, "I'll be back in ten minutes."

The enthusiasm in his voice told her he meant it.

Jace's dad, a big lumberjack of a guy, happily chatted as they walked along a stone path to the carriage house. Inside the spotless garage that housed two cars, one sensible sedan and another that looked like a race car, he led them up a set of steps and into a sitting room with a small kitchenette in the back.

"It's lovely," Marnie said, knowing from the expression on his face that he awaited approval.

An open door on the right led to a bedroom, as did an open door on the left. Their luggage had been neatly piled in the sitting room at the center of it all.

"Bathroom's back there." Jace's dad pointed to a closed door, equidistant from each of the bedrooms. "If you need anything, just tell me or my wife. We have anything you might have forgotten." He pointed at the bedroom to the right. "Crib's in that room."

His laugh was big and jolly as they thanked him, and he headed back to the party in the main house.

She glanced around. "This place is fabulous."

Danny frowned as he took off his suit coat, then his tie. "The suite?"

"No. The whole place. I'll bet they own acres and acres of that green grass out there."

"No, doubt," Danny agreed. "Here." He reached for Rex. "Let me get him settled."

For once she didn't argue. She grabbed her luggage and headed for the bedroom on the left. Tossing her biggest case on the bed, she glanced at the pretty blue bedspread and the lace curtains. Old-fashioned, but so comfortable and cozy, like stepping back in time.

She wondered what it would be like to have a family history. To have customs and traditions—

and a crest and plaid. But before she could think it through, Danny appeared at her door.

"Everything okay?"

"Everything's great."

He strolled into the bedroom. "Rex went out before his head hit the blanket."

"Travel makes some kids antsy and others sleepy." She slipped to the right, away from him, because it seemed so natural, so normal that he'd be in her room. And it shouldn't.

"Rex must be one of the kids that travel makes sleepy."

She nodded. "You go on back to your family. I'll sit here while he sleeps. That way I'll be only a few feet away if he stirs."

He nodded and headed for the sitting room door to leave, but as his hand reached the knob, he stopped, looked over at her.

"What?"

"I don't know. Everything just feels different here."

"Charlotte said it's enchanted."

He sniffed a laugh. "Yeah, she always says that as if there are fairies who grant wishes."

"So maybe you should wish not to be the family stuffed shirt? Maybe a passing fairy will hear, snatch your wish from the air and grant it?"

He laughed. "Really? You think I'm a stuffed shirt too?"

"I think you are practical and pragmatic, and I think the world needs that."

He shook his head. "Practical and pragmatic?"

"You think things through. You don't jump on bandwagons."

He groaned. "I *am* a stuffed shirt."

She laughed. "Go have fun with your family."

"I'll go but when I get there, I'm telling jokes and breaking out the good whiskey. I'm *not* a stuffed shirt."

Danny left the suite, bounded down the stairs and outside. Clean air filled his lungs, along with that sense that Charlotte talked about. He wouldn't call it magic. He would call it serenity.

He entered the kitchen to the sounds of laughter. He didn't have to ask about the good whiskey; apparently Jace's dad liked that a lot better than champagne. Some of the guests had drifted outside to enjoy the pleasantly warm evening. Some had retired to their rooms. Toddlers weren't the only ones who got tired from a long flight.

He took two fingers of whiskey and splintered off from the small bundle of people still chatting in the kitchen. He found a chair and settled in to enjoy the scent of the pond, the trees, the gardens all around.

"Mind if I sit?"

He glanced up at Mark. He wasn't Danny's favorite person in the world, but he refused to be considered the wet blanket anymore. If he had to talk to Mark, so be it. "No. Sure." He motioned to the other chair. "Sit."

"Penny's been riding my back about giving you a penthouse to live in, then keeping the elevator codes and showing up when I want to."

"She's not wrong."

He winced. "So, I'm apologizing and also promising it will never happen again."

Mark's unexpected apology and promise surprised Danny so much, he looked over again. "Thank you."

Mark shifted on his chair. "Okay. Now to the real reason I'm out here." He took a breath. "You haven't adjusted."

"Adjusted?"

"To being my son. To being wealthy. To any of it."

"I'm working on it." He chuckled. "I didn't get up and walk away when you sat down."

"Yeah, that's progress. But the girls adjusted so much faster. Within six weeks, Leni found a purpose. It took Charlotte more like eight, but once she realized she could be, have or do anything she wanted, she decided to use her construction expertise to help Leni and her free time to love Jace. It was simple for them both."

"You didn't humiliate Charlotte and Leni by making them attorney for your estate then faking your death."

"You're still mad about that? Because I didn't fake my death."

"Yeah. Yeah," Danny said, rolling his eyes.

"I didn't."

"Either way, you did make me attorney for your estate when I'm your *son.* Do you have any idea what an idiot that made me look like?"

"I do now. But back when I was setting it all up, I just saw it as a good way for you to get an understanding of my...*our*...holdings. To see everything with neutral eyes."

Danny sighed. "Whatever."

"Look, hiding you guys could be considered a mistake by some people but not by me. I had enemies and I had money. You were all targets."

Danny peered over. "And we're not now?"

"I've retired. Made friends with my enemies, and I have the best protection under the sun in Jace's group. It's why I couldn't leave Rex out there unprotected. When I learned about him, I knew other people could too. I had to get him under the umbrella. That was reason enough for me to come clean about everything."

"By faking your death."

"You've got to let that go, Sergeant Pepper."

"Sergeant Pepper?"

"Yeah, the guy with the Lonely Hearts Club Band."

Danny snorted.

"You're moping about something."

"Haven't you heard? I'm pragmatic and practical."

Mark laughed. "All I heard was stuffed shirt. And that was a joke. Who called you pragmatic?"

"Marnie. She was trying to make me feel better about the stuffed shirt teasing. She made me feel worse."

"Ah."

"What's that supposed to mean?"

Mark rose from his chair. "The biggest mistake of my life wasn't not being a part of the lives of my children. It was leaving the love of my life. I thought about Penny every day. Sometimes I out-and-out mourned the loss of what we could have had." He swirled the whiskey in his glass, then peered down at Danny. "Don't do that. Don't walk away from the woman you want. Do whatever it takes to keep her."

He strolled away without giving Danny a chance to argue, so all his wonderful retorts died on his lips.

With a growl of annoyance that Mark just couldn't seem to stop butting into his business, he started to lift himself out of his chair, but his parents came over. His mom sat. His dad looked around as if he'd finally found himself in heaven.

As much as he wanted to dislike Mark Hinton, seeing the happiness on his parents' faces, he couldn't.

Mark really was giving all of them things they never could have earned on their own. He was unselfish. He was easygoing. And to make as much money as he had, Mark also had to be smart.

Oh, who was he kidding? Everybody knew Mark Hinton was brilliant. Probably one of the smartest men of his generation.

And he'd told Danny to do whatever it would take to keep the woman he loved.

The thought whispered through his brain.

Tiptoed into his soul.

Did he love her?

If he did, did he want to be like Mark, alone and pining for the woman he loved, but couldn't have because his wealth separated them?

CHAPTER FIFTEEN

JACE AND CHARLOTTE'S outdoor wedding surpassed Marnie's expectations. The air shimmered with the enchantment Charlotte believed hung over the MacDonald compound. A beautiful bride in a long-sleeved lace gown that slid along her tall, slim frame, she gazed lovingly at her groom, who wore a kilt. Marnie could have sworn she swooned.

Then she looked from Jace to his brother Oliver, the best man, and to Danny, also a member of the wedding party.

No one was more handsome than Danny Manelli in a tux. With his hair neat and tidy, his bow tie tight and his white shirt crisp beneath his black suit coat, he was perfection.

His eyes moved and suddenly his gaze snagged hers. She sat on one of the white folding chairs facing the flower-covered arch where Jace and Charlotte said their vows, holding Rex. Wearing a little navy blue suit, he looked cute as a bug.

And Marnie had to say she didn't look so bad herself in a simple pink dress.

Her head tilted. Was that why Danny kept staring at her? Why he couldn't seem to break eye contact as his sister promised to love and cherish her new husband? Because she looked nice? Because she was mothering his child...

Or was there something more in that look?

A shiver wove through her, reminding her of the connection she'd always felt to him. It was almost as if he was trying to tell her something.

The ceremony ended. Congratulations and toasts to the bride and groom went on for an hour, as everyone at the small, private wedding felt entitled to say their piece.

Filet mignon and salmon cooked to perfection were served under a huge white tent. There were more toasts, dancing and cake.

Close to eight, Rex's bedtime, he fussed. It amazed Marnie how quickly he'd adjusted to the time change. He'd slept through the night and got up at six as he always did, but on Scottish time. Then he napped at two that afternoon and now he was tired at his regular bedtime. Surprised, but not one to go looking for trouble, she searched the crowd for Danny. Without making a ripple in the celebration, she motioned to him that she was taking the baby to their suite to check his diaper and give him a cookie.

He nodded.

In the room, she changed him into pajamas, found a cookie—or rather a biscuit, as Jace's mom called them—in the stash in the diaper bag and led him to the sitting room. He ate his cookie, laughed and played a bit, but she could see he was worn out. Two minutes after she put him in the crib, he was asleep.

Tired herself, she glanced at the TV in the sitting room but headed to her bedroom to get her pajamas and toiletries. Her hair piled on top of her head in a loose bun, she soaked in the tub for at least twenty minutes.

Feeling refreshed, she dressed in her pajamas, put her wet towel in the hamper, gathered her things and stepped into the main room, just as the suite door opened and Danny walked inside.

Seeing her, he immediately spun around. "I'm sorry."

She laughed. "Danny, I'm in very covering pajamas. You probably saw scantier clothes on the street last week."

"I know, but it's you."

Her heart skipped a beat. He'd said it as if she

were special, unique. Her feelings for him rose and tightened her chest.

"I respect you."

She swallowed hard, as new emotions swamped her. He'd said that before, but tonight she realized that though she'd never voiced it, she'd been angling for respect since the day her dad left, when she couldn't abandon her unconscious mom, and her dad had called her a traitor.

"Thank you." His words filled her with something that made her stand taller, even as her nerves settled. "But it's fine. Really. I was planning on watching some television." She headed for her room. "So, give me a minute to dress." She stopped suddenly and squeezed her eyes shut. He hadn't returned looking for her. Stupid that she would think that.

She turned to see he was already heading for Rex's room. "You're here to check on Rex."

"Yes...and no." He peered over his shoulder. "I'm really tired. I could use an hour of television to unwind and then about fourteen hours of sleep."

She understood what he meant. His family was wonderful. But they were also noisy and sometimes overwhelming. She couldn't ship him out there again just because she wanted to see what was on Scottish television.

"I don't mind having company while I watch TV."

He turned a little more. "I'd be very happy for the company."

Her lips lifted slightly. "Okay. You check on Rex. I'll put on yoga pants and a T-shirt and we'll be set."

He nodded and she went to her bedroom and changed out of her pajamas and into her usual nanny attire of yoga pants and a T-shirt. She looked at her hair and winced. If she fixed it, it might look like she'd done it for him.

If she didn't, it remained a mess.

So maybe better a mess than sending the wrong message? She liked him. She'd always liked him. But there could be nothing between them.

She left her hair in the sloppy bun and joined him in the sitting room.

In the back, making popcorn, his tux exchanged for a T-shirt and sweats, he turned and smiled. "What do you think we'll find on TV?"

She shrugged and plopped on the sofa. "Hard to say. Are you sure you don't want to be at the reception?"

"It's winding down. I told my parents I needed

to check on Rex, and I got a kiss on the cheek and an 'I'll see you in the morning,' then they went back to dancing."

He brought the popcorn to the sofa and she sighed. "Dancing. That looked like so much fun."

He gaped at her. "You should have said something! We could have danced."

She scrunched her face. "Not really."

"Marnie, there's literally no one here who cares who I am. Who *you* are. I think we should enjoy that."

She took a handful of popcorn, glancing around. The room was silent save for the muffled sounds of music and laughter coming from the MacDonald's backyard. He was correct. There was no one here but family.

"It's a wonder there's been no press here."

"Part of it was Jace's maneuvering. The other part though is that people in Scotland have known this family for generations. They don't think of them as wealthy. They think of them as neighbors."

She listened to the sound of the music from the wedding reception, interspersed with bursts of laughter. "You couldn't do this in New York City."

"Precisely. Which is why I think we should go somewhere tomorrow."

"Take Rex to see the countryside?"

"No. Take *you* to see a bit of the country. We won't have all day or anything, but I'm sure I can talk my parents into watching Rex for a few hours." He caught her gaze. "Enough time maybe for lunch in the village a few miles down the road."

She said nothing.

"Come on. No one will care, and I want so badly to do this." He took her hand. "Every time I look at you, there's this thing that builds in my chest. A longing. I would show you the world, if I could. But I can't. And I respect your wishes on that. But this is one time we can skirt the rules, be ourselves, and I want it."

Looking at their joined hands, feelings swamped Marnie. Memories of going to the art gallery, their first kiss, his standing up for her to her dad, her thank-you kiss and making love. Now they were sitting here like two normal people and the emotion running through her was hotter, deeper, than the things she felt in the high points of their relationship. The connection that wove them together filled her with such yearning her heart almost burst.

She wanted it too.

"Only if your parents don't mind watching Rex."

He slid his arm along her shoulder and nestled her against him as he leaned back on the sofa. "There are four or five couples who'd be happy to keep him."

She leaned into him, taking a handful of popcorn and reveling in the simplicity of the moment. "I suppose."

"So, don't overthink it."

"I won't."

Suddenly, in the quiet, secluded room, the past didn't matter. She sank deeper against him, breathed in his scent. Refusing to let her brain race back to the memories that always haunted her, she closed her eyes and simply enjoyed being with him.

Everything felt different in the car on the way into town. Last night, after a chaste kiss goodnight, Danny had gone to his room, knowing this was what he wanted. A little time with her. Not necessarily to persuade her that they could have something together, but if the opportunity came up, he wasn't going to let it pass unused.

He'd thrown on jeans and a T-shirt with tennis

shoes, working to look as completely unlike a wealthy person as he could. After breakfast with the family, he'd also gotten permission to use the sedate sedan in the carriage house. As he and Marnie zipped along the country road, looking at rolling hills with mountain backdrops, where he was and what he was doing finally hit him.

It might not have been a normal date, but it was a date.

Marnie also wore jeans, but she'd topped hers with a pretty pink shirt that brought out the red in her hair, which she'd left down. Thick tresses flowed around her shoulders and to her back.

Delicious feelings tumbled through him. Simple longings that mixed heart and soul and made him tongue-tied, unsure. If he could, he'd catch her hand and keep her with him forever. But she had doubts—about him, his life. About her past. Most of the time, he didn't even know how to address those, let alone assure her that none of it mattered. Because in Manhattan it did. He wouldn't lie to her and pretend it didn't.

Still, he had a few glorious hours. To be himself and let her be herself. Simple American tourists.

Who liked each other—

"You looked really nice yesterday in that pink dress."

"I better. I paid enough for it that I'll be wearing it to the next six weddings I go to."

He laughed. Naturally. Easily. Not just because he'd been middle-class enough to understand stretching a dollar, but because he could. No one knew him here. No one knew her. That's how he'd enticed her into spending a day with him.

They could literally do anything they wanted.

"I think we should look at today as an adventure."

She laughed. "Seriously? Unless you've found a hoard of Vikings to fight, I think it's going to be a normal morning."

"Hey, I'm trying to make this work." As soon as the words were out of his mouth, he knew he'd made a poor choice.

Her gaze shot to his. "I don't want you to have to *make* it work."

"Actually, that's our problem. We've never had to make it work. When we're together, alone, not thinking about who I am or who you are, it does work. That's been our trouble from the start. It worked so well we forgot about boundaries."

She fought not to close her eyes and remember the night they'd made love. Because he was correct. Everything they did felt right. Every time she looked at him, she had the sense that he was hers. Hers to love. Hers to laugh with. Hers.

But that was a pipe dream. Her subconscious longing for something it couldn't have. It made her curse fate at the same time she questioned her sanity. She knew better than to fall for someone so far out of her league—

"You're overthinking."

She ran her hands down her arms, warding off the cold that suddenly filled her. "I guess I was."

"If we do that, we won't enjoy the day and I want to enjoy the day. To be myself again if only for four hours."

His words hit her in the heart. All these weeks of worrying about herself, she'd forgotten what Mark had stolen from Danny. A normal life. A chance to climb the ladder of success to earn and deserve his achievements. The possibility of meeting someone on a street or in a coffee shop, falling in love without worry of motives or their past.

She sucked in a breath. She, of all people, should want him to have this little space of time to be himself, not Mark Hinton's son, not one of the Hinton heirs. "You're right. Let's enjoy the day."

They stepped out of the car into a space so

quaint and wonderful it seemed they'd walked into a fairy tale. A small, old village, it still boasted cobblestone streets that looked to be as old as time. Shops could have been gingerbread cookies, iced with colors that made roofs, doors and windows with curtains.

"Wow! It's so beautiful."

Danny sucked in some air. "And quiet."

He wanted the quiet. She knew he did. But he needed more. In the same way that she longed for the ability to make a real human connection, to love someone without fear, he needed some time without worry. No stress. Only simple happiness.

She could give him that. Easily. As naturally as breathing.

The idea simultaneously thrilled and scared her. If she let her guard down, she knew what would happen—

But wasn't that what she wanted too?

The first time they'd made love had been rushed by overwhelming need. What would it be like if they took these few hours of privacy and did what they really wanted to do?

Bliss.

Memories.

No. More of a touchstone for her. The kind of memory she could point to and say *that's* what it's like when I'm free. When no one cares. Not even me.

The thought of having that memory wove through her. Not a temptation, but a necessity. Something to hold on to.

She definitely wanted this.

Sliding her arm beneath his, she cuddled close, hoping to warm his blood, to make him feel the need that tiptoed inside him and sent nudges to touch her, to kiss her, to just follow through on whatever he wanted.

"Let's go shopping."

Expecting him to say something romantic, she blinked, then peered at him. "What?"

"If nothing else, let's get souvenirs."

Her eyes narrowed. That was about as far from the afternoon she thought they both wanted as he could get. "You mean like get T-shirts?" She frowned. "My mom might want one."

He nodded. "I think my assistant would too."

She said, "Okay," and Danny let her lead them down the street. They eased in and out of the local shops. First buying T-shirts, then Marnie buying crazy things. Knitted scarves. Rain boots. Things that made him laugh. But when they came to a shop dedicated to menswear and she zeroed in on the kilts, she decided she'd found the way to give him a more direct clue that everything had changed.

CHAPTER SIXTEEN

DANNY FROWNED AS she pointed at the row of kilts. "You should have worn one yesterday. Jace and his brother did."

"I'm not Scottish."

She ignored him, sliding kilts along the rack until she found one that resembled the plaid of Jace's family. "You should try it on."

"Are you kidding?"

"You'd need a white shirt…" She rummaged some more. "And this sash."

He gaped at her. "No!"

Her voice dipped and she leaned in closer. "I think you'd look incredibly sexy."

His heart fell to his stomach. She'd never flirted with him before, always been too careful. "If you don't stop that, I'm going to kiss you right here."

Her eyes lit with mischief. "Well, for once, you're allowed, correct?"

She was right. No one noticed them. No one knew or cared who they were.

He moved in swiftly, didn't give himself time

to think, just let his lips meet hers, linger sweetly for a second, then go in for what he really wanted. The desire. The heat. The arousal that raced through his blood and set his nerve endings on fire.

Remembering they were in public, he pulled back, bumped his forehead to hers with a laugh. "Why'd you do that?"

"To push us to where we really wanted to be. We have one day." She shook her head. "No. We have a couple of hours. I don't want to waste them being polite. I just want a taste of what it would be like if we didn't have to care."

His inner self suggested he take her to a hotel, to ravage her, to give them both what they really wanted. But there were no hotels in the small town. Instead, they made the twenty-minute drive back to the carriage house and pulled inside the garage.

"What are we doing?"

"Jace and Charlotte left for their honeymoon today. All the parents went with them to see them off. My parents told me about it when they agreed to watch Rex. They said they needed the car seat so he could go too."

She licked her lips. "We're staying here?"

He opened his car door, stepped out. "Yes,"

he said as she got out of her side before he could open her door for her. "But there's a lock on the suite door and one on each of our bedrooms."

She finally got it. "Ah…"

They made short order of the steps, and once inside the cozy suite he locked the door. Before she could say anything, he pulled her to him and kissed her, long and deep, looking inside himself for that place of slow-build passion. There'd be no rushing this time.

He let his hands roam her back, ease her closer to him. He knew they didn't have all day, but they had hours. Hours to themselves. Something they'd never had. And he intended to enjoy it.

He slipped her pretty pink shirt over her head and tossed it to the sofa. She reached for his shirt, but he was faster.

She smiled. "I thought we had a few hours?"

He winced. "We do."

"So, what do you say we put on some nice music, maybe go to your room and talk—"

He hauled her to him and kissed her greedily. She laughed, but she was with him all the way. He walked backward to his room, kicked the door closed, locked it and fell with her to the bed.

He tried to slow them down twice, but there always seemed to be a ticking clock. Still, when she was warm and naked beneath him, everything decelerated to a crawl and he let himself savor. He took in her face, her sparkling eyes, the curve of her mouth and let them imprint themselves on his brain.

The fact that he felt the need to create a memory sent a shaft of sadness through him. He forced it aside, running his hands down her torso, luxuriating in the feel of her hands on him.

The sense of time standing still filled him. The feeling of eternity. The essence of forever. He relished it. Let it waft through him like a warm summer breeze before the need rose swift and sharp and they tumbled on the bed, each fighting for supremacy. He won, pinned her hands to the pillow and joined them. But the attitude of forever trembled through him again. For as much as he liked her sweetness, he also loved her sense of whimsy, balanced by her seriousness about Rex, about schedules, about them. She was small and soft and, oh, so warm. Sensual. Subtly daring. Fun. Interesting.

Longing filled him at the same time that they reached the peak. The word *mine* roared through him, along with a contentment so fierce he believed he could reach out and touch it. He could be anyone with her. A sharp lawyer. A single dad. Even a crazy billionaire's son. Being with her made him realize Mark, his job, even how he and his adoptive parents mended their relationship were all secondary to having her in his life.

He thought all those thoughts and feelings would disappear when they were cuddled together, drowsy, ready for a nap even though they'd probably have to get up soon and dress for when Rex returned.

But none of it disappeared. The feeling of completion, of accepting who he was and wanting her to be part of it wouldn't go away.

He told himself it was wrong.

He told himself he was going to be disappointed.

But he couldn't stop the happiness or the surety that he could make this work. Then he kissed her, and she laughed and the sense that this would last forever overwhelmed him to the point that he forgot how quickly time was passing and that his parents would be home with his son.

He took them to the place of passion and need quickly, easily and completely. They both rode the wave, longer this time, so that the end was deep and fierce. Stronger than any he'd ever felt. Sending the word *mine* through him again, and again, and again.

He barely had enough time to get his breathing under control when his phone rang. He gave himself a second to simmer down, closing his eyes, before the phone rang again.

Rolling to the side, he picked up the phone, saw it was his dad and answered. "Everything okay?"

"Yeah. You know, since Rex is fine, the group decided we'd get lunch."

"The group?"

"Everybody just piled into a couple of limos to see Jace and Charlotte off at the airport. The MacDonalds mentioned a place up the road, a B and B that serves lunch and dinner and we thought we'd all go there."

"Rex will be tired at two."

"We should be back by three."

Danny smiled at Marnie. "Good enough."

He disconnected the call, glanced at the clock and rolled over to kiss Marnie. "We have two hours."

She laughed. "Want to go back to town and get lunch?"

"Maybe." He flopped down on his pillow, enjoying the feeling of her skin skimming his as she settled beside him. "But first I just want to do nothing for a few minutes."

She levered herself on her elbow, so she could

look into his eyes. Her hair fell across her shoulder. Her beauty took his breath away. The ease of their connection, the easy contentment, always amazed him.

"When was the last time you took a vacation?"

He snorted. "You sound like Mark."

She ran her hand along his chest, sending soothing chills down his spine. "Which isn't such a bad thing from my point of view."

He gaped at her. "Really?"

"Yeah. I mean, I definitely get that he's out there. And I absolutely understand how what he did embarrassed you. But I see him pulling your family together."

His eyebrows rose.

"I'm serious. He's included everyone. He doesn't act like he's supreme, almighty biological dad who doesn't want the adoptive parents around. He wants everyone around. He wants everyone to be whole and happy."

He remembered the joy on his parents' faces the day before. "My mom and dad would have never visited Scotland had it not been for Mark."

"And I'll bet they will be going to Paris next month for the wedding."

"They are."

"Sometimes when I look at your family, I see

a puzzle. There are five hundred scattered pieces and you guys are the ones who have to figure out where they fit. Mark brought you all together. He's giving you every opportunity to simply enjoy it. But you guys are the ones who have to make the picture."

He thought about that for a second. It was exactly what Mark had done. And it was exactly what he, Charlotte and Leni had to do. Make the picture.

A sense of wonder tiptoed through him. Not just the rightness, but the perfection of Marnie. How she understood him. He'd never met anyone he wanted as much. Never had this feeling of a partnership before.

He caught Marnie's shoulder and brought her down for a kiss. "When did you get so smart?"

She laughed. "I have always been smart. I just don't get the opportunity to use my smarts very often."

Because of her past. Because she hid. She was an excellent nanny, but she could be so much more. She knew it…

And it hurt her.

For the first time, he saw that in her eyes.

And he cursed it. Without Mark's money, he wouldn't have thought twice about dating her.

No one would have cared about her past. But now they had to. He wouldn't care if a reporter did a huge write-up about it, but she did, and he would swim the deepest sea, fight the biggest battles to protect her.

Even if it meant staying away, when he wanted everything.

The thought filled him with indescribable loss. Emptiness so deep, his soul blackened as if lost in a storm.

But there was no shelter. For the second time in his life, he had no idea what to do. He'd been gobsmacked when he'd discovered Mark Hinton was his dad, and he'd floundered. Now he wanted Marnie but there was no open door. No way to make it work.

And the loss felt like one from which he'd never recover.

The truth of the thought brought him up short. Forced a decision he never thought he'd make. He couldn't let this be a loss.

He'd fight for this.

They flew home the next day, and Marnie had never been so depressed to see Manhattan. They settled Rex in the limo that awaited them at the private airstrip, silently drove to Danny's building and got out as quiet as two church mice.

Danny carried Rex to the elevator. Marnie followed behind, her head down, her thoughts going a million miles a second. What had felt like home when they left now felt cold and empty. Scotland had been full of people and fun. Green grass. Big blue sky. Wide-open spaces with no media. People she could talk to without worry. Fun dinners.

And love. Danny hadn't said the words, but she'd felt it in his touch. They'd slept together in her bed that night. Not for sex, though that had happened naturally, but to be close. Gloriously close. Connected. Secure.

To return to a building with a doorman and bodyguards and millions of people with a phone was a potential disaster. No matter how beautiful the penthouse, it was a prison.

The driver carried up their luggage. Instructing him to leave the luggage by the elevator with a wave of her hand, Marnie told him they would take care of separating it and getting it to the appropriate rooms.

When he was gone, Danny laughed. "Do you see how easily you just gave orders to your bodyguard?"

She walked over and into his waiting arms. "I thought he was Rex's bodyguard?"

"Doesn't matter whose bodyguard he is. You just gave him orders." He dropped a quick kiss on her lips. "But in a way that's good because I wasn't sure you'd be happy if I told him to take your bags to my room too."

She pulled back. "Seriously?"

"You don't want to sleep with me?"

She wanted to *everything* with him. She simply wasn't sure how long it would last. And every time she thought that, her chest hollowed out. Her breaths hurt. Still, that was a worry for another day, wasn't it?

She peeked up, met his eyes and smiled. "You know I do."

He kissed her and she returned his kiss, but the sound of Rex pounding on his highchair tray reverberated through the open space. They broke apart and she walked into the kitchen.

"Did Daddy forget to give you juice?"

Danny walked in behind her, slid his arms around her waist and pulled her back against him. "You know with the time difference he's going to be ready for bed soon and sleep all day."

She turned in his arms. "I'll handle it. I'll let him sleep long enough this morning that he's got some energy, then give him his usual nap this afternoon and, voilà, he'll be ready for bed at eight."

He laughed and he kissed her. "You're such an optimist."

"No. I'm just really good at what I do."

"Okay, then I'm going to change and head to the office."

She nodded. "We'll be fine."

Danny's smile said he knew that. Because they had bodyguards and security protocols in place.

And maybe she was being ridiculous?

They could be anyone they wanted behind the closed doors of his penthouse, and that's what she should focus on. That happiness. That joy. And not worry about the future.

CHAPTER SEVENTEEN

DANNY WAITED TWO weeks for Jace to return from his honeymoon with Charlotte. He walked into the spare, but adequate workspace Jace maintained as a home base for his staff and was immediately ushered back to Jace's private office. Decorated with modern furniture in coral, aqua and beige, the place was almost beachy. Until Danny sat on one of the chairs.

"These are the most uncomfortable seats in the world."

Jace laughed. "I know. It keeps visitors' stays to a minimum." He leaned back in his obviously comfortable desk chair. "What can I do for you? You said it was urgent. Something happen with Rex?"

"I'd like you to investigate Marnie."

He came to attention. "Why? What did she do?"

"It's not something she did. It's what she told me."

"Something from her past?"

"Yes."

"High school?"

"Yes."

Jace leaned back again. "We already know."

"You do?"

"Of course, we do. You don't think I'm going to let someone near Mark's grandson without knowing every little detail of her life, do you?"

He squeezed his eyes shut. "I was hoping you wouldn't be able to find that."

"It was an easy leap, Danny. Her name seems to appear out of nowhere when she turns sixteen and enrolls in high school. But she had records from another high school. We quickly realized she'd begun using her mother's maiden name. We found her mom's married name…realized her dad was Eddie Gouse. Followed that name and, voilà, there she was."

"So you know what happened to her?"

"Yes." Jace sat forward again, put his arms on his desk and said, "Danny, she's a good person. No trouble. But from what I've read, women who go through that kind of harassment can end up with post-traumatic stress disorder. Her mother got her out of the situation very quickly, but who knows the impact of being violated that way."

"She worries."

"That the pictures will come forward?"

"That it will ruin her life." Danny pulled in a long breath. "And your team being able to dig up her past so easily doesn't help."

"Maybe just don't tell her that we know."

"I was going to use you not being able to find anything as a way to convince her that she shouldn't worry."

One of Jace's eyebrows rose. "Worry about dating you?"

Danny rose. "And other things."

Jace stood too. "Danny, she's a really, really nice woman. But if she can't face this, she's not the one for you."

Not the one for him? He wanted her. Wanted everything they had in secret. Casual happiness. An easy, loving relationship. He could not let her get away. He had to find a way to make this work.

"She's faced it once. She shouldn't have to face it again."

"Yeah, but she's never been under the kind of media scrutiny she'd get as your girlfriend."

"So, it's my fault?"

"Actually, if you're going to place blame, put it on the ill-mannered teenage boy who took the pictures. Or Mark for making you a celebrity of a sort."

Danny fell to his seat again. "I've just started

to make my peace with Mark. But I don't want this position anymore. I don't want to be an heir. I don't want to be a Hinton."

"You can't go backward." Jace sat too. "That was Charlotte's big plan. She'd renounce the estate and return to being a vice president at her development company. But that's not how it works. The press would be even more interested in someone who refused billions of dollars."

"We could move to Scotland."

Jace laughed. "And they'd find you. They'll always find you if you're part of a delicious story. Frankly, you're less interesting as someone who accepts he's an heir and takes the money."

"Except for Marnie."

"Except for Marnie."

Danny drew a long breath. "I hate everything you just said."

Jace put his hand on his chest. "Hey, I don't make the rules. I just know them and know how to work with them. I can tell you exactly what's going to happen here. If the press gets suspicious, somebody's going to start poking, the way they did when Leni first got here. All it takes is one person to find one thread. To go to the high school in the school district for her mom's apartment, the one she's rented for over fifteen years, realize Marnie *Olsen* just appears one day—but with transcripts from another school that doesn't have a Marnie Olsen—which means she used another name, figure out who her dad is, look under Marnie Gouse and, voilà. Once a smart reporter or investigator gets her name…she's out."

Defeated, Danny rose.

Jace leaned back again. "Want my advice? Put the story out yourself. Control the narrative."

"She shouldn't have to face this again."

"But she does. That's life. And the only way to get ahead of it is to put the story out yourselves."

When Danny stepped off the elevator of the penthouse, his eyes met Marnie's and she knew something was wrong. Not only was it midafternoon, and he normally didn't get home before six-thirty or seven, but also his usually bright eyes were dull. Listless.

She walked over and kissed him. "What's up?"

He stepped back, away from her and the first level of panic hit. "I could use a drink." He strode to the wall bar tucked behind the piano. "You want a drink?'

She ambled over to him. "I'm on the clock."

"One drink won't hurt."

"Okay, now you're scaring me. What happened?"

He set his empty glass on the bar. "I talked to Jace today."

"Oh, that's right! He and Charlotte are home from their honeymoon."

"It wasn't a cheery visit. I asked him to investigate you."

Mouth open, she fell to the teal-colored sofa. "Oh."

"I wanted to see how difficult it would be for someone to uncover your past."

That was actually a smart, positive step. "Okay."

He closed his eyes and let his head fall back. "He knows. He's always known."

A weird sensation bubbled through her. Her past and her present met. And not kindly. It left the room cold, the conversation awkward. "Well, that didn't take long."

"I don't know how long it took. He said he couldn't trust the care of Mark's first grandchild to someone unless he knew everything about her."

"And he let me stay?"

"That's a point in your favor. He didn't let you stay because he likes you—though he does. He let you work for me because you aren't the bad guy. You were the victim."

Everything he'd said was good. Which meant there was more. "But—"

"But he believes there's trouble on the horizon if the press finds out."

Relief rippled through her. "Of course, there is. But the press isn't going to find out."

"Jace thinks they are. Maybe not today or tomorrow but eventually and you'll have to face this."

Her blood froze. "Face this?"

"He believes the only way around this is for you to come out in the open with it."

"That's ridiculous. I'm your nanny. How silly will it look for me to call a press conference or give an interview?"

His eyes met hers from across the room. "Not silly at all if we wanted to come out in the open about our dating."

Her frozen blood stopped flowing. "No."

"Marnie, just listen. I'm trying to figure this out." He walked over, sat beside her. "I want this so bad I can taste it. We're good together naturally, easily. You know as well as I do that what we have doesn't come along every day."

She squeezed her eyes shut. That had always

been her touchstone—that what they had didn't come along every day. That's why she savored it, wrote in a journal, pressed certain memories into her heart. She wanted to have all of this to remember.

Danny rose unexpectedly. "We don't have to make a decision today. And no matter what we choose, Jace will be with us every step of the way."

Marnie's breath returned. Her lungs filled with air. Her world righted. "Okay."

He walked into the kitchen as if totally back to normal. "Paris is next week. Is there anything I need to do to help you get ready?"

She rose from the sofa. "No. I have everything under control."

"Only staying a weekend makes a big differ-ence."

"Yeah."

He reached for his phone. "What do we want for dinner?"

She shrugged. "I don't care."

"I'd love a steak." He pursed his lips. "But I don't want it delivered. Too bad we can't go out."

His words sent a shaft of fear into her heart as the reality of their situation hit her. He would eventually tire of having to tiptoe around her life. And she wouldn't blame him.

He brightened suddenly. "I know! Let's get Italian."

"I love spaghetti."

"Me too."

And just like that her fears disappeared again. But the sense that she'd witnessed the beginning of the end of their relationship lodged in her brain. Not because Danny was a demanding guy or even impatient. Because there was no future. People had relationships in secret because there was no way to come out into the light. And Danny and Rex deserved light. Light and love and laughter that they didn't have to hide.

They arranged to have dinner delivered at seven, so Rex could help Marnie eat her spaghetti. When Rex went to bed a little after eight, Marnie shoved her fears away. If this was all the time she got, she refused to waste a minute fretting about the future.

They slept together, made passionate love, but for Marnie there was a ticking clock. An end. A vibrant, attractive, interesting man like Danny wouldn't live a lie, have a secret.

In fact, the one thing they'd both forgotten was that Mark Hinton's lie, his multiplicity of secrets, had already ruined Danny's well-planned life. It was no wonder he was trying to get them out from under her past. Once he realized that what they were doing was no better than what Mark had done, he'd be gone.

Or he'd ask her to go.

He wouldn't be able to live a lie.

Wouldn't live under the shadow of secrets.

CHAPTER EIGHTEEN

EVERY DAY BECAME SPECIAL, important to Marnie. She cuddled Rex a little more, loved Danny a little harder and didn't make weekend visits to her mom's anymore. Judy didn't mind. Having loved taking care of Wiggles while Marnie and Danny were in Scotland, she'd gotten herself a dog. A big, mixed-breed variety, Charlie walked her mom, instead of the other way around. In a fragile sort of way, everyone seemed to be happy, moving on with their lives.

As the little jet Danny had been assigned flew into Paris, she could see the Eiffel Tower, and an unexpected peace filled her lungs with air. Out of the country, where no one really cared about the Hinton family, the trip would be glorious.

With no property large enough of his own to use as a family headquarters, Mark had booked two floors of a luxury hotel. As in Scotland, Marnie and Danny were assigned a suite with Rex's crib in Danny's room.

She entered the sitting room with a gasp.

"Wow." Drapes were open, revealing a view of Paris that stole her breath. Bowls of white roses sat on every table. Plush rugs covered hardwood floors. White sofas sat across from each other, with white club chairs beside the table in front of the window.

Danny looked around. "There is no denying that being rich has its perks."

She laughed, taking Rex from Danny's arms, so she could get him ready for his nap. "What's on today's agenda?"

"Nothing. There's not even a rehearsal dinner. Mark said the ceremony will be simple. As his best man, I'll stand beside him with the ring. Charlotte will be her mom's maid of honor, and Leni will do a reading."

"We can do anything we want tonight?"

"Yep. Sightsee. Have a nice dinner out. Take a walk along the Seine."

"I'm getting Rex on France's time. What's going to seem like afternoon to us will be his bedtime."

"That's okay. I've arranged for my parents to watch him tonight."

"You have?"

"Don't worry. They figured things out long ago.

Most of the family has." He caught her gaze. "Are you okay with that?"

Everyone had always treated her more as a friend than an employee. "Yes. I mean… I suppose we do have a certain glow."

He laughed, then caught her up for a quick kiss.

His parents arrived at eight o'clock Paris time, actually one o'clock in the afternoon, New York time. She gave them the instruction to let Rex sleep but Danny's dad all but shoved them out the door. "Go! Have fun! We got here two days early. We got most of our sightseeing in. Rex is in good hands."

Walking down the hall, Marnie said, "Coming a few days early was smart."

"My dad has been with his employer a long time. He has oodles of vacation time. I don't."

The elevator came and they stepped inside. "You could if you went to work for Hinton, Inc."

He groaned. "That's not going to happen."

"Okay, then don't be jealous of your dad's many vacation days."

Danny laughed and shook his head. "Let's just focus on our own stuff. Like the house that's in escrow down the street from theirs. There's absolutely no furniture and I sold my condo furnished. So that's a big job that'll be waiting for us after we close."

She sighed. "That's a lotta house to furnish."

"We can hire a decorator."

They stepped out into the warm Paris night. The scent of pastries drifted around her. The streets were crowded with tourists and residents of the world's most romantic city.

"Hiring a decorator seems cold. Impersonal."

"I'm glad you said that because my mom asked if she could help get the place organized."

"I think that's a great idea."

He took her hand, turned her to the right, and they began walking up the street. "You do?"

"Sure. That house is all about cementing your adoptive parents' place in your life. She's your mom. Moms usually like a part in things like this."

"Then it's settled?"

"Yes." And she felt good about that. She felt good in general. The night was perfect. Not a cloud in the sky. She was with a man she adored. His parents seemed to like her. "Where are we going?"

"Restaurant's just a few blocks up the street. I thought you'd like to walk."

"I would." She glanced around. No one was

looking at them oddly. No one was really looking at them at all. "Where's the bodyguard?"

"Outside the hotel, watching Rex."

"Good idea."

He slid his arm across her shoulders and nestled her close. "The best idea. There's nothing like being in the most romantic city in the world with the woman you love."

It took a second for the words to sink in but when they did, she stopped dead. "You love me?"

"You don't love me?"

Their gazes met. Her past tried to overshadow her, but she was in Paris. The man she loved had just told her he loved her. *In Paris.* She refused to let her past ruin this moment.

Warm fuzzies filled her. Dreams that she didn't even realize she had came into focus. Her eyes filled with tears.

"Yes. I do."

He caught her by the waist and hauled her to him, kissing her deeply. She remembered every second of the kiss, the habit of memorizing every detail so engrained that it happened automatically. She cataloged the feeling of his lips, the way their bodies met, the warmth in her soul—

And a little voice whispered, *You don't have to give this up.*

She didn't want to. It cut her to the core to think of moving on to protect her secret.

So, don't think of it. Test the waters of believing this is your future.

Even the thought was scary, but they broke the kiss, their gazes staying connected, and she felt what her soul was trying to tell her. This was it. Danny was the man she was supposed to spend the rest of her life with.

The question was… How?

No answer came, but throughout the night she noticed that no one paid them any mind. Danny's last name, the name on his credit and bank cards was Manelli. Not Hinton. When he paid for dinner or pastries at the little café just a few blocks down from the restaurant, his name aroused no curiosity. As they strolled along the Seine, passersby smiled politely but no one knew who they were… Who *he* was.

Like Scotland, no one knew who he was. No one cared who he was.

A plan began to form. A simple one. Danny wasn't ready to leave his job at Waters, Waters and Montgomery yet. But he would be one day. The whole world had opened up for him, and someday—with no restrictions to bind him—

he'd realize he could be, have or do anything he wanted, the way Leni and Charlotte had.

And when he was ready, she would suggest that they move to France or Spain or get a vineyard in Italy.

Suddenly, their future opened up to her. The life she wanted. The life she could have.

And she knew moving was the answer.

Mark and Penny's wedding was held at the Musée Rodin. Penny looked spectacular in a short white dress with a skirt of tulle ruffles and a short veil. Mark was resplendent in his tux. The wedding party posed for pictures around the manicured grounds, inside the museum, with Rodin's sculptures sometimes, sometimes without.

Danny did not give a flying fig that the pictures took forever, the wedding planner was like a drill sergeant or that Rex was cranky. The night before, Marnie had been different.

His.

Totally his. No hesitation. No fear.

He could feel it in her touch. He could sense it in the way she fell into a deep, peaceful sleep.

So he'd made a plan. He'd decided to talk to Jace again when they returned to New York. They'd find a sympathetic reporter, someone who would know how to tell Marnie's story correctly, and they would come out.

Just the thought filled him with relief. Dancing under the stars, they'd laughed more than usual. She hadn't held back or hidden her feelings for him around his ever-growing family. Charlotte had beamed as if she were the matchmaker who'd set them up. Leni had smiled knowingly, reminding them that the family was meeting in Mannington, Kansas on Christmas Eve and she expected them to be there.

It was the best night of his life.

When Rex couldn't stay awake even a moment longer, his parents volunteered to take him back to Danny and Marnie's suite. They loved the elaborate, elegant wedding, but they loved Rex more.

Danny and Marnie stayed, dancing until the band quit. Then they took a limo to the hotel.

This time, when they stepped out of the car, she saw a gaggle of guys huddled together beside the door, smoking.

Odd for such a high-class hotel.

When Danny turned from helping her exit the limo, a rumble went through the group. They spoke French so the only word she understood was Danny.

At the sound of his name, Danny caught her

elbow and hurried her inside the hotel. Out of the corner of her eyes, she saw their driver, Danny's bodyguard, walk up to the entrance and stand in front of the door. As if guarding it.

Of course, he was guarding it. That was his job.

When the elevator doors closed behind them, she said, "What was that?"

"I'm guessing someone recognized me."

Fear raised gooseflesh along her arms. "Recognized you or was waiting for you?"

He took a breath. "My entire family is here. For all we know they were waiting for Charlotte. She's the pregnant one. The interesting one."

The elevator doors opened. "But they knew who you were."

He motioned for her to walk down the hall. "I'm going to say that they didn't know who I was. They took a guess and got lucky."

Which was why they hadn't raced to follow him inside. Her fear subsided. They hadn't known for sure he was Charlotte's brother.

Relief sighed through her as they entered their suite and though she didn't forget what had happened, she put it to the back of her mind. But when they returned to Manhattan and exited the limo in front of their building, there was no guesswork among the reporters.

"Danny! Danny! Mr. Manelli!"

Marnie unbuckled Rex from the car seat and pressed him to her as she raced to the door.

"How was the wedding!"

"Is Mark happy?"

"Do you like your new stepmother?"

They entered the building to the sound of questions. None of the reporters was foolish enough to follow them, but Jace's men closed in on the door, standing in front of it.

As the elevator door shut behind them, Marnie turned to Danny and just gaped at him.

He sighed. Staring ahead, at the elevator door, he said, "The wedding might have been a secret, but Mark released a statement that he'd gotten married before he and Penny left for their honeymoon." He ran his hand along the back of his neck. "The reporters were just curious."

He peered at her. "And not about you. They barely saw you. They were curious about Mark and Penny."

The elevator door opened, and she stepped inside the penthouse. Realizing she was still clutching Rex, she loosened her hold but a thought hit her. She was holding him like a mother, not like a nanny.

Reporters weren't going to assume she was the nanny. They'd think she was Rex's mom—

Or Rex's stepmom—

At the very least Danny's girlfriend.

Her heart sped up. Her fears washed over her like a bucket of cold water.

Danny took Rex. "This doesn't have to be a big deal."

"It *is* a big deal."

"But it doesn't have to be." Carrying Rex, he led Marnie to the sofa, then sat beside her. "I talked to Jace for a minute at the wedding. I told him that I realized the wisdom of the advice he'd given me the day I went to his office to talk about you. I told him I agreed with him. That I totally understood that we needed to get ahead of your secret with an interview. He said he knows a hungry reporter who'd do just about anything to get the story."

Her heart stopped. "You talked to Jace? Again?"

"After you said you loved me, it all came together." He shook his head. "Marnie, you have to know we can't go on living like this."

"I thought we'd move to France…or Belgium or Spain or an island in the Pacific."

"My work is here. My life is here."

She licked her suddenly dry lips. "Danny,

you're not going to stay at Waters, Waters and Montgomery. Even if you don't want to work for the family, you can be anything you want. Work anywhere you want."

"No! I won't give up my job. That's the only solid piece of me I kept from my old life."

"That and your parents—"

"Who aren't really my parents. My relationship with them is back to being good, but it will never return to what it was. I'm different now. My profession—*that choice* is the only part of me that's me." He leaned back on the sofa, taking Rex with him. "I never put all that into words before, but it's true. I didn't wake up one day and say I wanted to be a lawyer. I worked to figure it out. I busted my butt in law school to be the best. It is like an anchor now—who I am."

"And my secret is who I am." Her words came out soft, discouraged. Because this was their real problem. As much as it felt like they meshed, their lives didn't.

He caught her hand. "Your secret might be part of your past, but it isn't who you are."

"Isn't it? It guided my career choice, caused me to change schools, kept me in the background no matter how much I wanted to leap forward."

"And now all that's going to end. With one succinct conversation with a sympathetic reporter."

She closed her eyes as the feeling of finality squeezed her chest. "It doesn't matter if the reporter is the most sympathetic person in the world. There are a million reporters and bloggers and podcast people who will jump on the bandwagon, speculate, call me names…"

"You can't go on living a lie."

"I don't live a lie. I have a secret."

"But if you told that secret, it would lose its power over you."

She shook her head, imagining being mobbed on the street, seeing her own picture in tabloids, not even being able to buy a pastry without someone looking down his nose at her because no matter how clear she would be about what happened, people would embellish. It would be like high school all over again but a million times worse. And this time she wasn't the only one who'd be hurt…

"No. No! I can't do this."

Rex fussed, crawling up on Danny's shoulder. "Let me put him down and we'll talk about this."

"No." She rose as he rose. "To me there is nothing to talk about."

"Not even the fact that you love me, and I love you?"

She looked him in the eye. This time she didn't want to remember what she saw there. Pain. Confusion. And maybe a little anger. She didn't blame him. She was angry too. But when she saw herself talking to reporters, getting questions shouted at her about the night she lost her virginity or why there'd been a bet on who would get her virginity, her skin crawled. She remembered the bullies. The kids who'd thought it all nothing but a game and ruined her life. Reporters would consider it their jobs to get the truth—no matter how ugly. No matter how much it was none of anyone's business.

She took a breath, fought back the torrent of images, found the strength to speak without tears.

"I always knew it was going to end. I just didn't think it would be this soon."

He caught her hand. "Give me a minute to put Rex down for a nap. I'll be right back. We can make a plan."

She smiled slightly but didn't nod her head or verbally agree. She had enough trouble in her life. She didn't need to add lying to it. When he returned, he would want to discuss outing her and she just couldn't do it.

She'd be sixteen again. Alone. Vulnerable. So fragile she'd shiver every time she stepped out her front door. While vultures picked at her bones. Not caring if they shattered her.

As soon as Danny reached the nursery, she headed for her room, quickly packed her meager belongings and was gone.

Her phone rang a hundred times that night. Danny left at least ten text messages. She deleted them all without reading them.

He was better off without her.

In fact, his life would be good without her.

The truth of that shattered her.

CHAPTER NINETEEN

MARNIE WOKE THE next morning to the sound of
traffic. She opened her eyes, saw her old bedroom
at her mom's apartment with the window raised
to combat the late September heat.

Tears filled her eyes. Her empty soul billowed
in the breeze left when everything she wanted
had been yanked away. Her heart and mind were
like a ghost town.

She sat up, positioned herself to rise, but she
couldn't. *This* was the moment she'd spent her
life fearing. The time when her past would rise
up, albeit privately, and cost her her future.

*She hadn't yet saved enough money to start
her business.*

*She'd lost the man she loved. The child she
loved.*

*There was nothing to look forward to. Nothing
to hope for.*

*These walls and temporary nanny jobs were
her future.*

Nothing more.

The noise of the apartment door opening rent the air.

She squeezed her eyes shut.

And she was back to living with her mom.

Her door suddenly slammed open and her mom's monster dog raced in, jumped on her bed and knocked her down. Judy flew in behind him.

"Charlie! Sit!"

The dog just looked at her.

"I'm telling you. Obedience school did not work."

Marnie gave Charlie a quick pet before she nudged him off her bed. "He just needs more lessons."

"We don't have the money."

"You can have the money I saved." She lay down in the bed, a solid ball of misery. She didn't have enough to start her business, and probably wouldn't get another job with an inflated salary like the one Danny offered. There'd be no nanny business for her. "It doesn't matter anymore."

"Oh, it's pity party time."

She sat up, gaping at her mother. "Look at the pot calling the kettle black."

"I told you rich men were trouble. I warned you. But no. You had to go to Scotland with the guy, then Paris! You got a taste of all the money and things and then you thought you were in love."

"I didn't think it, Mom."

"Sure. Sure. You fell solidly in love in three months...with a guy so far out of your league you probably didn't even really have anything in common. Sure. I buy that."

Disgusted that her mom had it all wrong, she toyed with a loose string on her worn bedspread. "Don't worry. It's not like I thought it would last. I knew it wouldn't, so I saved most of my salary."

Judy eyebrows rose. "Really? Most of your salary?"

Marnie laid back on her pillow. "I had an exit plan."

"I thought I had an exit plan with your dad too—"

Her disgust returned, rising up so unexpectedly Marnie didn't have time to combat it. "Mom, this is totally different! You and Dad were married. I worked for Danny."

And I love him.

Thinking that made it hurt to breathe. She'd barely said it to him. Realizing that now only hurt worse.

"I have enough of a past that I knew I had to be smart. I didn't let my thoughts go any further than that. You taught me that. Taught me not to dream."

Judy's face fell, as if Marnie had slapped her. "Oh, Marnie!" She pressed her fingertips to her forehead. "No. I never told you not to dream. I was warning you to be careful."

"Well, I was," she said, unexpected anger pouring through her. Her parents' marriage had been a mess. Her mom herself had been a mess for decades before she finally pulled herself together. And right now, Marnie didn't want anybody preaching at her. She'd finally, finally found what she wanted, a man she could spend the rest of her life with—and she couldn't have him.

She didn't need anyone reminding her that she'd lost something she'd never really had. She'd lived the last ten years with the knowledge that most good things would slip through her fingers.

"I am always careful, Mom." She fought the tears that wanted to form in her eyes. She refused to give in to the misery of it. She'd long ago accepted her fate.

Judy shook her head. "Okay. I'm seeing something here that I don't like."

Marnie cursed her mom's therapist for always phrasing things as if she were in a session.

"I never told you not to dream."

"You never told me I could dream either, Mom."

"It's not the same thing."

"Of course, it is!" Regret rattled through her. "And you can tell your therapist I said that. Because, you know what? Splitting hairs the way we always do, looking for the path of least resistance was great, but it caused me to stagnate."

"I don't think you stagnated! I see lots of progress in your life. You got your degree. You had a great job. Hell, you said yourself you have a plan."

But she didn't really have a life. She had a plan. Always a plan. Never a real sense that she was living. Only existing. Never the feelings she'd had in Scotland or Paris, where everything was simple and beautiful. Never the glorious freedom of being with the man she wanted more than her next breath of air.

The agony of his loss broke her, but when it did, something wild and bold poured from the cracked shell of her soul. In the same way that fear had always paralyzed her, this thing—this *courage* rising out of the ashes of loss—seemed to give her life and energy.

Charlie tried to leap on her bed again. Judy cried, "Charlie, no!" She grabbed his leash from the floor with a heavy sigh. "I'll take him to the kitchen, get him a snack so you can get up and get dressed."

Her mom left with Charlie, closing the door behind her, and Marnie squeezed her eyes shut. Without Danny, *this* was the rest of her life.

The courage that had puffed out of her soul whispered through her again. She hated this life. Always had. But she suddenly wondered if her mom did. Judy had always blamed being shoved into high society for ruining her marriage, and Marnie had simply thought that was an excuse for her drinking.

But what if she *had* hated high society life?

What if she'd feared being in the spotlight so much that she shrank from it with alcohol? She'd cleaned up rather easily once she'd been out of Eddie Gouse's life. And had stayed sober as long as she was hidden—

And what if that's what she'd taught Marnie?

That she'd only be safe if she was hidden?

Marnie pressed shaking fingers to her forehead. What if she'd handled her entire life, the big high school mess, all wrong by hiding from it?

Danny wasn't surprised when Mary Poppins, real name Mary Grant, had shown up at his apartment the night before. She made short order of getting

Rex to bed, liked the list of rules and hints Alisha had provided and got herself set up in the room that had been Marnie's—

He squeezed his eyes shut. Even thinking her name hurt his chest.

He couldn't believe she'd left without telling him, then wondered why that had surprised him. Revealing her secret would be painful, awful and oh, so public. Why would he be surprised that she'd run rather than even discuss it? He'd called a hundred times. She hadn't answered once.

He forced himself to go to work, settled in his seat behind the big desk and told himself that having the weight of Marnie's troubles lifted was a good thing, but he knew it wasn't true. He might be able to replace her as a nanny, but he'd never connected with another human being the way he had with her.

The things he'd told her the night before about her life being a lie rumbled through his brain like thunder, and he took a long, slow breath. She didn't really lie. She hid. But in a way, wasn't that the same thing? When a person hid, technically, they were putting on a show, pretending, lying about everything.

The thought froze his brain. He didn't want to

believe she didn't love him. If she lied about that, something inside him would die.

He knew it.

He didn't feel like quite the idiot he believed himself to be when Mark Hinton announced he was his biological dad and all the progress he'd made at his job, all the promotions, all the accolades were actually the partners of his firm sucking up to their biggest client. Still, thinking through Marnie's life, he felt sorrier for her than he did for his own loss.

What they had had together was amazing, and the loss bruised his soul, but her loss was worse. She'd never had a normal life. A normal *anything.*

His heart broke for her, but just as quickly he forced himself to think about work. Think about documents. Do something good for one of his clients.

The pages swam before his eyes. Not from tears, from exhaustion. He hadn't slept the night before, torn between going after her and staying right where he was. If he went after her, persuaded her to tell her story to a reporter, it wouldn't be her choice, her idea. He'd always wonder if he'd forced her hand. If things got bad, he'd be the culprit who'd convinced her to do something she hadn't wanted to do.

The choice had to be hers, and when she'd left his penthouse, she'd made it.

And now he was tired. Tired. Hurt. Gutted.

He picked up his phone and called Nick. "Hey, Dude."

Nick snorted. "Danny? Did you just call me *dude*?"

He laughed. "I'm exhausted today."

"You must be if you let loose with a *dude*."

He took a breath. "Look. I was thinking I'd like to get away with Rex. I want to go somewhere quiet and serene. I need a break."

Nick chuckled. "Yep. I knew this was coming. At some point you all fall apart. There's no shame in this, Danny. Finding out Mark is your dad was hard enough. Finding out you were adopted, your job was a setup—those hurt. Add back-to-back weddings in Europe and, yeah, you need a break." He paused. "Let's see. There are mountain cabins, a little cooler now that it's the first week in October or there are island retreats. Still hot. But quieter because kids are back in school and summer vacations have officially ended."

"Heat and sun sound good."

"My recommendation? The house in the Florida Keys. There are Jet Skis and fishing boats. We even have a captain on retainer… Let me look. Yep. There's a guy to drive the boat so you can drink beer and fish."

"I think I'd like that."

"Okay, then, give me two hours to get a jet ready."

"That's about how much time I'll need to get Rex and his nanny packed—if she'll go."

He laughed. "Marnie enjoyed Scotland and Paris as much as we all did."

Danny's breath caught as he realized no one knew Marnie was gone.

Nick casually said, "How long are you staying?"

With thoughts of Marnie still washing through him, living without her, having the park, the bakery, even his home remind him of her, Danny stayed silent another second. When he spoke, it was quietly. "Not sure. Maybe forever."

His heart officially broke as he said those words. But he was so tired. So awfully tired of the circus his life had become since Mark had entered his world. Clinging to his job hadn't helped. So he'd leave his job. Take his child. Go off the grid.

And never think of Marnie Olsen again.

Marnie's next assignment was nannying the twins of a very sedate banker and his pediatrician wife. She had a moment of pride when Dr. Sponsky told her she was doing everything right. That she was the first nanny Shirley had sent her who didn't need coaching.

So, she was good. On target. The pay wasn't as high as working for a Hinton heir—which was how she referred to Danny, so she didn't have to think his name and have pain swallow her for days. And though she was in the same neighborhood, she'd heard he'd moved. Gone to the Florida Keys. Charlotte hadn't been able to let Marnie go onto her next assignment without an explanation, so she'd called and that had been awkward.

But here she was, the first of December, eight weeks after the great loss, in the park where she'd walked Wiggles, now pushing a stroller with twin girls. Two cute-as-a-button sweethearts.

She rolled the double stroller up to her usual bench, turned it so she could talk to her darling girls and sat.

"So, good day today, right?"

Nine-month-olds, they could only babble. But she loved it. Sheila was a little more expressive than Sandra. She knew a few words. Nothing like Rex—

She stopped the painful thought. Rex had become like her own child. If she let herself think of losing him, she'd splinter again. And she couldn't do that. Not again. Not anymore.

She tucked a blanket around Sandra. The day wasn't freezing, but there was a chill in the air.

And she did not think about the Hinton heirs. Ever.

She leaned back, enjoyed the sun that poked through the clouds, enjoyed the final leaves that had fallen from the trees, dancing around her in the breeze, and started counting the months it would take to save enough to have first and last months' rent on a tiny place she'd found. Knowing how much her mom's opinions had impacted her, Marnie couldn't live with her anymore. She hadn't said anything. Didn't want to hurt her mom, but she had to get out on her own. Be herself. Figure out who she really was.

The apartment might be taken by the time she had the necessary cash, but the landlord had said he had another one opening up first of the year. Renter was a deadbeat. Couldn't pay the monthly allotment.

She stopped the rush of sympathy for the girl. Marnie was poor too. And she got weekends off. She needed a place—away from her mother. Though, truth be told, now that she had Charlie,

Judy Olsen was a lot less negative. She actually went out. Had friends—

"I see you're back."

Damn it! Her father.

He hadn't been here any of the other times she'd brought the twins to the park. Why now?

He snorted. "Twins this time? You switch jobs like I switch underwear."

She gaped at the stupid old coot. "Then you must not change your underwear very often."

He laughed, plopped down on the bench and opened his newspaper.

Of all the unfair things that had happened to her in her life, having him for a father was the one thing she didn't have to let hover over her head. It was what it was and he shouldn't be allowed to spook her.

"You know what, old man?" She called across the space that separated them, causing both of the twins to look up at her. "You shouldn't laugh at me so much. You're partially responsible for who I am."

He lowered the paper. Scowled at her. "How do you figure that?"

She bounced off the bench. "Because you're my dad. You left *me* when you left my mother. You refused to see me when I came to try to make a connection. You had a maid tell me to leave. And this is who I became. So, get off your high horse. You're partially responsible for me."

He stared at her. "Marnie?"

She stood tall, defiant. "Yes."

He set the paper on the bench and rose as if bemused. "Oh my God."

She grabbed the stroller handles. "Yeah, amazing, right? I knew you probably lived around here somewhere. I just never realized we'd run into each other so damned often."

"Only a few times." He studied her. "I don't know what to say."

"You don't have to say anything. I wouldn't have told you who I was if you hadn't annoyed me so much. I don't want you in my life. Don't want anything from you. Except a peaceful visit to the park."

She set the stroller in the direction of the Sponskys' condo. "So, if you see me here, don't come in. And if I see you got here first, I won't come in."

She left him standing openmouthed in front of his bench.

But as she strolled her babies back to their home, she couldn't help remembering the shocked expression on his face. He'd been numb.

A chuckle rose.

It didn't just feel good to stand up to him. It felt good to tell him who she was—

His daughter.

The enormity of admitting that almost paralyzed her, and she stopped pushing the stroller. She was a child who'd been abandoned by a wealthy man, who'd gotten confused in her teen years, looked for love all the wrong ways—

And had been victimized.

She'd been victimized.

She wasn't the criminal here. She wasn't the one who should be hiding—

Her breath stuttered.

Danny was right.

He was always right.

Her eyes filled with tears, but she laughed through them. It had taken her weeks to realize he'd had the plan—she had to come clean. But that could only happen after she'd faced her first demon. Her dad.

Now that that was done, she wanted it all to be over.

All.

Of.

It.

She wanted her life back.

She pulled her phone out of her pocket. Hit a speed dial number.

"This is Marnie Gouse Olsen. I'd like to speak with Jace, please."

CHAPTER TWENTY

MARNIE WALKED THROUGH the lobby of the Trusik Building, home of Lancaster Media, her head high, adrenaline pumping through her. Jace followed her. Not discreetly as he normally did, but beside her like a friend, not a bodyguard.

They took an elevator to the appropriate floor, spoke to a receptionist and were guided to a small space that looked like someone's living room. A young, hip producer attached a mic to her collar, then walked away.

Two minutes later, Angelica Cabala ambled over. Tall and slender, with long red hair, she read some note cards.

When she reached Marnie, she extended her hand to shake Marnie's. "Ready?"

"Actually, the sooner we start the better."

"Great." Angelica nodded once. She straightened in her chair, then faced a camera. "And we're back," she said, as if they were just returning from a commercial break, when they were actually taping this segment to air the next morning.

"Today, we have a special guest. This is the woman who used to be the nanny for Danny Manelli's son, Rex. As anybody who's turned on the news lately or read a newspaper knows, Danny is missing Hinton heir number three."

"Welcome, Marnie."

The camera panned to Marnie. Her chest froze. Her stomach fell. But she thought about Danny. How much he'd been through for her and how she'd run—even though she'd promised herself she'd never run again.

She sucked in a breath. "Thank you."

Angelica opened her delicate hands with finger-nails adorned with green nail polish that matched her dress. "Let's get right to it. You called me and told me that you and Danny had a more personal relationship than employer and employee and that you had a story to tell."

Jace had told her that admitting the personal relationship was the quickest, best way to get a reporter to sit up and beg for her story. And he'd been right. Angelica had invited her to come to the studio immediately.

"So, I'll ask the question that's on everyone's

lips… Seriously? A nanny falling for her boss? Isn't that a bit of a cliché?"

Danny had told her that. It was his first defense against their attraction. The memory of the day in the park lifted her lips into a goofy smile. Everything she felt for him when they were together tumbled through her.

"Actually, we both acknowledged that right off the bat. We did not want to be a cliché."

"Yet, here you are."

"We may be a cliché to you, but we aren't to each other. You know Danny's world had been turned upside down. The lives of all three of Mark's kids were upended."

Angelica's perfect eyebrows rose. "You call realizing you're filthy rich upended?"

"Leni, Danny and Charlotte all had life plans. Leni had parents she loved. Danny didn't even know he'd been adopted."

That reminder sent sadness rippling through her. He'd been going through so much and she'd hurt him. She hadn't said goodbye. Too afraid he'd talk her into something that she wasn't ready for.

She raised her head, straightened her spine. "It's like winning the lottery. Everybody thinks it's wonderful. Everybody sees the good side. But there's another side."

"So poor little rich kid?"

Anger sputtered through Marnie. "No. And you know that." She glanced around. "You didn't just one day get dropped into this studio."

Looking affronted, Angelica said, "I worked my way up."

"And had years to adjust."

"Well, yes."

"The Hinton heirs didn't. From day one of their discovery, they've been followed. They've been in the news. If they didn't have such good protection, I'm sure people would have gone through their garbage."

Folding her hands on her lap, Angelica leaned forward. "And what about you?"

"I was the nanny mostly for young, upwardly mobile executives. I'd never worked for someone so wealthy." She looked into the camera. "And I made mistakes."

Angelica's smile grew predatory. "Mistakes?"

"You said yourself a nanny and an employer getting involved is a cliché."

Angelica said nothing.

Marnie swallowed. It was now or never. Do or

die. She couldn't handle that she'd hurt Danny. Couldn't handle another day of being afraid.

"I changed my name, ran from my past. Because of a predator."

Angelica's eyebrows rose to her hairline. But again, she said nothing, giving Marnie the chance to say something explosive.

Marnie took a breath. "Someone took pictures of me in a compromising position." She shook her head. "No. He took nude photos. When my mom called the authorities, I was the one villainized, harassed, bullied. I wasn't running from the person who took the pictures. He was told to delete them, and I believe he did. In ten years, there's been no evidence that he didn't. What I ran from was bullying."

Angelica blinked. Looking speechless. She didn't know what Angelica had been expecting, but clearly this wasn't it.

"I won't run anymore. And I won't hide. If the pictures show up because I'm involved with one of the richest men in the world…so be it. That's life." She glanced at Jace. "A good friend told me that I'm undoubtedly not the only person this has happened to and maybe I needed to set an example for how to handle it."

Angelica's face scrunched. "So, you're facing it head-on?"

Marnie nodded. "Yes. All of it. The fear. The running. The secrets."

"That's admirable." She set her now-useless note cards on the table. "That's powerful."

"Not powerful. It's real."

"Yes. It is. And you're right. It's probably a story shared by hundreds, if not thousands of other women. Do you see yourself as a crusader, a leader who will help other women?"

She shrugged. "Everybody has to handle this in their own way. I simply got tired of hiding, of being afraid. Maybe I'll inspire someone else to come forward, but really most women don't have to. They just have to give themselves permission to stop being afraid."

"Again. Powerful words." Angelica leaned forward, squeezed Marnie's hand. "Marnie, thank you for being here."

"Thank you for letting me tell my story."

"We're out of time, but I'd love to have you back to hear about your life with Danny Manelli. Hear about the world of the Hintons."

Marnie laughed. Her secret wasn't a secret anymore. The weight that had been lifted was incomprehensible. The most delicious thought trickled through her. *She was free.*

"Thank you, but no." She wasn't really in the Hinton world anymore. She'd hurt Danny. Exposed the Hinton family to public humiliation and embarrassment…and more press. As if the media needed a reason to hound them.

Angelica waited another few seconds, maybe hoping Marnie would say more. But she didn't. This time, though, she wasn't keeping a secret. She was being discreet. The difference between the two was sanity.

When the director said, "Cut," Marnie reached for her mic. Angelica breached the distance between them. "I mean it. Anytime you want to talk, I'm here."

Marnie said, "I'll think about it." Then she walked up to Jace, who accompanied her out of the studio, then out of the building.

Even before Jace's limo dropped her off at her mom's apartment, Shirley called. She'd been fired by the Sponskys. No one wanted a celebrity as a nanny. Shirley knew this notoriety would fade away in a week or two, but the Sponskys didn't.

She'd lost yet another thing—a good job.

And lots of parents might not want to hire her.

The step that was supposed to fix her life had actually broken it even more. The relief of not having a secret ebbed into reality. Everybody knew her. She was a broke, famous nobody.

Two weeks later, with no jobs coming her way, she got the news from Shirley that there was a long list of employers who didn't want her.

She nodded, though tears filled her eyes. She crawled into bed that night with her mother tucking her in.

"I'm telling you. This too shall pass."

"Another saying from your therapist?"

"Nope. That one's in the good book."

Marnie shook her head. "I'm fine."

"Sure. Sure. We're always fine."

"You know that money I've been saving to get my own apartment?"

Her mother's eyebrow rose. "Not really, but go on…"

"I think I might have to move to another city." She'd thought of that the night she'd officially become Rex's nanny. It had made sense then. It made more sense now.

Her mom pressed her lips together, then whispered, "Yeah. You might." She rose from the bed. "Good night, Marnie."

She could hear in Judy's voce that she regret-
ted the way things had turned out. She caught her
mother's hand. "It's not your fault."

"Thanks, but some of it is."

"How about if we just say it is what it is and go
forward from here?"

Judy smiled. "I'd like that."

"Me too." She'd lost her dad, lost her job, lost
Danny and Rex. She didn't want to lose her mom
too. Now, that they were both aware of the mistakes, they could heal together.

After a restless night, Marnie woke the next
morning to pounding on the front door. She
waited a few seconds for her mother to get it.
When she didn't, Marnie called, "Ma! Get the
door."

The pounding increased, and no sound came
from the main room of the apartment. With a
groan, she threw off the covers, slid her shabby
robe over her pajamas and marched to the door.

Stupid salesmen!

She yanked open the door and there stood
Danny Manelli.

"Hey."

She gaped at him. Her heart sped up to a million beats a second causing her pulse to race and
her thoughts to scramble. "Hey."

"Can I come in?"

She looked back at the poverty she called home, remembering that she'd made a firm choice not to run, not to hide from who she was. She and her mom barely had enough money to pay the rent. But that was her life. Her truth. She wasn't running anymore.

"Sure." She motioned for him to enter. "Come in."

He looked fabulous in his camel-colored overcoat. His hair dotted with snow. His black leather gloves in his hands instead of on them. "Rex misses you."

She smiled as she thought of the toddler who'd loved her. The little boy who was so easy to love in return. Blinking tears from her eyes, she said, "I miss him too." She walked to the coffeemaker. "Can I get you something to drink?"

"No. What I have to say will only take a minute."

So, he was here to say his piece. Maybe yell at her for leaving so abruptly. An arrow plunged into her heart. Now that she was down, it seemed everyone wanted to kick her. She was surprised her father hadn't called. He knew who she was. It would be a simple thing for him to track her down. After all, he had resources.

"I saw the interview."

"I thought you were in Florida." *And wouldn't see.*

"I was. But my sisters saw it, and I called the station and they sent me a video."

She winced. "I should have thought that through. Jace had said that dropping hints about our relationship would get me the interview. The chance to come clean publicly, so I wouldn't have a secret anymore. It was a bad time for me." She combed her fingers through her hair. "A mess. I didn't think it through. I'm sorry."

"You sort of hinted that your feelings for me weren't gone."

"Hinted?"

"You don't have a poker face, Marnie." He laughed. "Your expression said a lot more than your words. But you started the interview talking about us."

Her gaze jumped to his. *No more lying. No more hiding.* "Yeah."

"So, telling me you love me in Paris… That was true?"

"Yes."

"And leaving without a word, not answering my calls that night… What was that?"

"I thought I was protecting you. From me. My past. My mess."

"It's what Jace thinks."

She squeezed her eyes shut. "You talked to Jace?"

"Yes. He's squarely on your side in this."

She laughed sadly. "He's a good guy. I'd have never gotten through this without him."

"And Charlotte would have shaken him silly if you hadn't gotten through it."

Charlotte. She pictured her round and pregnant. Leni cheerful. Mark and Penny newlyweds. She missed them all.

"I guess you're going back to Florida?"

He looked at her. "It's no fun without you."

Her heart stumbled. Her lips trembled as a million wishes pounded in her brain. But she wasn't the kind of woman who got wishes. Wasn't the kind who put herself out on a limb.

"I also don't think I can ever go back to Scotland again. I'd see you everywhere. That wouldn't be any fun either."

She pressed her lips together, blinked to stop the tears from spilling from her eyes.

"Unless you went with me."

She laughed. "Might as well. Nobody else wants to hire me."

"Oh, I don't want to hire you either."

Her head snapped up. "You don't?"

"It's what got us into trouble the first time."

"Yeah."

"I'd really like to marry you."

This time, when her heart stumbled it was with hope. The words tried to sink in and almost couldn't. She'd hurt him, hurt herself. She was a mess.

"No answer?"

She passed a hand through her hair. "My life is in shambles. Not something you should be getting involved with. Don't say things you don't mean."

He faced her. "I mean it. Watching you on that video." He shook his head. "That was the bravest thing I've ever seen."

"You think so?"

"Yeah. And crazy as this is going to sound, I liked that you didn't do it for me. You did it for yourself."

She swallowed hard.

He opened his arms. "Come here. I love you."

She raced over, threw herself against him. "I love you too. I think I always did. But it was so much."

"Too much," he agreed before he kissed her.

They broke apart slowly and stared into each other's eyes. "I actually do live in Key West now."

"Charlotte told me."

He laughed. "She does like being the link that keeps us all together." He kissed her again.

"What about Waters, Waters and Montgomery?"

"I didn't really want to work for them as much as I simply wanted to practice my craft. Believe it or not, there's a market for good lawyers in the Keys. But I don't have to deal with crazy, fighting families. I write wills, help with property transfers, write a lot of agreements for the businessmen who want the same thing I do—peace and quiet and the ability to fish when I want to."

She laughed.

"I love it there. Would you care if we lived there?"

She laughed. "Sun and warm weather all year round... And you and Rex? I'd love living there too."

"And maybe we can get married in Paris?"

"I liked Scotland. You think the MacDonalds would let us use the compound?"

"I think they're family, and they'd be happy to have us."

"So, it's settled. Another wedding in Scotland."

"Another wedding in Scotland." He peeked at her. "Next summer?"

She stood on her tiptoes to brush her lips across his. "Next summer." She grinned. "Get a kilt."

He threw his head back and laughed. The sound echoed through the small apartment and followed them to the limo and the airstrip where his private jet awaited.

When they were in the air, Marnie sank into the plush seat and closed her eyes.

This was the rest of her life. And it would be a good one.

No more fears.

No more worries.

No more secrets.

EPILOGUE

DESPITE THE HEAVY snow falling on Mannington, Kansas, on Christmas Eve night, the Hinton family's smallest jet made a safe landing at the private airstrip. Marnie bundled up Rex for the walk from the airplane's steps to the limo Jace had waiting, as Danny grabbed the handle for Wiggles's carrier.

He groaned. "We've got to buy him diet dog food."

"Don't be silly. He's a Lab. He's growing."

They stepped out into the big, fat, fluffy flakes that fell around them, creating a winter wonderland.

"I can see why Leni doesn't want to leave here."

Marnie looked around in awe. "Yeah. But this cold white stuff will get old in a week or two. I like the ocean. The sun."

When they reached the limo, Danny opened the door for her. It was one of the compromises they had found. They needed to be able to do simple, normal things for themselves and each other.

Before Marnie slid Rex into the car seat, she removed his big coat, fastening him into the seat wearing only his hoodie. Danny had already gotten the sermon on how big coats can leave the harness too loose. So, he said nothing, just followed her into the car when Rex was secure.

"Nervous?"

"About seeing your entire family again?" She laughed. Wearing a black wool coat with her auburn hair tucked under a thick white knit cap and a matching scarf wrapped around her neck, she looked like she was prepared for frozen tundra, not a snowstorm in Middle America. "I did an interview that caused every person in Manhattan to know who I was. I've handled worse than the six sets of parents at your sister's house."

He took her hand, kissed the knuckles. "You've been very brave."

She laughed. "Stop teasing."

He couldn't help it. He loved hearing her laugh. There'd been something about her from the very first second he'd met her. Something that had drawn him. On the deepest level, he'd known he'd fight heaven and earth to keep her, and in some ways he had.

The limo driver took them to the door of the huge house Nick and Leni had built. Danny pulled the hood of Rex's sweatshirt up to cover his head and raced inside, Marnie on his heels.

They stepped into the high-ceilinged foyer, open to almost the entire first floor amid a cry of "Merry Christmas!"

Removing Rex's hood, Danny said, "Merry Christmas!" as his family poured over to hug Marnie first, then him. As always, someone took Wiggles's crate to let him loose and someone scooped his son away from him. This time it was Penny.

"He's so cute!"

"You're going to have your own cute grandchild in a few months."

A round, pregnant Charlotte grinned. Jace shook his head, laughing.

Penny glanced at Danny. "Technically, Rex is my grandson too… Step-grandson." She winced. "Good gravy, we have a lot of family."

A laugh erupted from the group. Leni's adoptive parents, Danny's adoptive parents, Leni and Nick, Nick's parents, Charlotte and Jace, Mark and Penny—

And Danny and Marnie. It had almost taken a miracle to get them together.

As if reading Danny's mind, Mark slipped away from his new wife, over to Danny. "Thank you for coming, son."

For the first time, having Mark call him son didn't send blistering anger crackling along Danny's nerve endings.

He glanced at Marnie, who'd removed her coat and walked into the kitchen area. She took one of Leni's cookies, bit into it, and her face filled with bliss. Going through what she had, had shown Danny the realities of what Mark had been facing every time he'd brought a child into this world and made him see the validity of Mark's fears.

But Marnie had also taught him to count his blessings, see the good before the bad. Not care so much about how or why and simply enjoy the life with which he'd been blessed—

He'd go through it all again, because she'd been worth it.

And this reunion, the huge family created by parents, adoptive parents, kids and of course Penny and Mark, might be the payoff Mark had always lived for. A time when he could be with his kids, have the family he'd longed for, finally be a real dad.

"You don't think I'd miss Nick and Leni's Christmas Eve party, do you—" he glanced around, then caught Mark's gaze "—Dad?"

Mark's eyes filled with tears. "That's the best Christmas gift I ever got."

Danny clasped his shoulder and maneuvered him in the direction of the kitchen area, where everyone had gathered around a baked ham, homemade rolls and so many cookies Danny was sure no one could count them. A huge Christmas tree decorated with white lights and red bows sat by the fireplace in the adjoining family room, and Christmas carols played softly in the background.

"Oh, so you don't want the watch I bought you?"

Mark sniffed. "I think I have forty of them."

Danny threw his head back and laughed. All animosity, all confusion, wiped away.

As Penny ambled to the big center island with the promise of a cookie to Rex, with Leni and Nick taking drink requests while Jace talked on his phone handling a teeny-tiny problem with a rock star who wanted Tiffany's opened because he forgot to get his mom a gift, Danny joined Marnie by the platter of cookies.

He slid his arm along her shoulders. "Welcome to the rest of your life."

She cuddled against him. "It's going to be an adventure, remember?"

He laughed. "Yes. It is."

* * * * *